"Let's get married. You and me."

Mick's expression went from dumbfounded to completely horrified in a matter of seconds. "Woman, have you lost your mind?"

Ignoring the direct hit to her ego, she said, "Perhaps. But if that's what it takes to protect Sadie, then so be it."

Standing, he crossed to where she stood. "Christa, I appreciate what you're doing here, but you can't marry someone you don't love."

"Oh, as if there aren't plenty of married people who don't love each other. And I wasn't talking about moving in together or anything like that."

"No, you were thinking of a little girl who's been tossed around by enough of life's storms. And I admire you for that. But I would never dream of tying you down in some marriage of convenience. You're a beautiful, spirited woman who deserves to love and be loved."

Christa knew Mick was just being nice, that her suggestion to get married was totally ludicrous, yet staring up into his green eyes, she found herself wondering what it might be like to be loved and wanted by a good, hardworking man like him.

It took **Mindy Obenhaus** forty years to figure out what she wanted to do when she grew up. But once God called her to write, she never looked back. She's passionate about touching readers with biblical truths in an entertaining, and sometimes adventurous, manner. Mindy lives in Texas with her husband and kids. When she's not writing, she enjoys cooking and spending time with her grandchildren. Find out more at mindyobenhaus.com.

Visit the Author Profile page at Harlequin.com.

A Brother's Promise

Mindy Obenhaus

LOVE INSPIRED
INSPIRATIONAL ROMANCE

LOVE INSPIRED®

INSPIRATIONAL ROMANCE

Recycling programs
for this product may
not exist in your area.

ISBN-13: 978-1-335-55423-9

A Brother's Promise

Copyright © 2021 by Melinda Obenhaus

This edition published by arrangement with Harlequin Books S.A.

For questions and comments about the quality of this book,
please contact us at CustomerService@Harlequin.com.

Love Inspired
22 Adelaide St. West, 40th Floor
Toronto, Ontario M5H 4E3, Canada
www.Harlequin.com

Printed in U.S.A.

Delight thyself also in the Lord;
and he shall give thee the desires of thine heart.
—*Psalms* 37:4

For Your glory, Lord.

Acknowledgments

Many thanks to Leonard Peters
for putting up with my multitude of
legal questions. You are a patient man.

Michelle Courtney, thank you
for your real estate insight.
I greatly appreciate all of your help.

Chapter One

Christa Slocum had to expand her hardware store before Crane's Building Supply infiltrated the area. And this might be the ticket.

A cold rain fell outside as she stood near the paint counter Wednesday afternoon, contemplating the brick wall Bliss Hardware shared with the vacant building next door. Not even a gust of wintry January air someone ushered in could jar her from her thoughts.

Bliss Hardware was a fixture in the small Texas town and under her ownership, the once sleepy little business was now bursting at the seams. But if she could take out those bricks to create an opening, the two spaces would be joined, nearly doubling her space and allowing her to add the home improvement section people had been wanting.

Giddiness bubbled inside of her. This was

the best option she'd come up with so far and it was so simple she wondered why she hadn't thought of it before.

Eager to contact her real estate agent, she turned and nearly ran into Mick Ashford, local rancher and good ole country boy. Except he wasn't a boy. He was a grown man, maybe a year or two older than Christa's forty-three years, with gorgeous light green eyes and the kind of rugged good looks that had many of the town's single women acting like fools whenever they were anywhere near the cowboy.

As far as Christa was concerned, though, he was simply her neighbor. Well, he lived in the house nearest to hers, anyway. A cabin tucked in the woods, far beyond the old farmhouse that had once belonged to his family. Until he and his sister, who lived near Austin, sold it to her.

At the moment, though, he stood in front of her wearing a Carhartt jacket and mud-spattered Wranglers, his chocolate-colored felt cowboy hat in one hand while the other fisted a color chip he must have snagged from the adjacent paint display. Deep lines she wasn't used to seeing creased his brow, suggesting something had him troubled. Which might explain why he hadn't razzed her yet.

"What can I help you with, Mick?"

"I need a gallon of this." He held out the paint swatch.

One glance and her brow shot up. "Mick Ashford, what could you possibly want with Pepto-Bismol-pink paint?"

"It's not for me." His tone was more serious than she was used to. "It's for Sadie. I'm hoping it'll make her feel more at home."

Sadie? Christa wasn't aware that Mick was dating anyone, or that he'd gotten married. Like Christa, he'd always been comfortable being single. But if he wanted to make someone feel at home, that could only mean someone else had moved in with him.

If so, it must have been a whirlwind romance. She could only hope it wasn't some woman he'd met online then proposed to after only a few dates. Because while Christa may not be interested in Mick, she considered him a friend and didn't want to see him hurt by someone with less-than-honorable motives.

"I guess you haven't heard." He watched her curiously.

"No." Which, given how small Bliss was and the fact that she owned a business many of the townsfolk frequented, was rather unusual. "I haven't seen much of you since Christmas." They shared a driveway, so she usually saw him in passing at least once a day. But he'd disappeared right after Christmas. Even had someone else checking on his cattle.

"I reckon I should have let you know I was leaving, but it was pretty sudden." He rubbed the back of his neck with a calloused hand. "And these last few weeks have been a blur."

Christa hoped he wasn't planning to tell her some long tale about his love life. "The holidays can do that to us."

His green eyes were filled with sorrow as they met hers. "My sister and her husband were killed in a helicopter crash in Colorado right after Christmas."

Remorse mingled with grief to squeeze Christa's heart. "Oh, Mick, I'm so sorry."

Clearing his throat, he simply nodded. She could only imagine how raw his emotions were. "Sadie is my niece. Jennifer and Kyle left her in my care."

And she thought he'd gotten married. Now her heart went out to the man who was obviously struggling. Mourning the loss of his sister while being thrust into the role of caretaker for a child.

She rubbed her suddenly chilled sweatshirt-clad arms. "How old is Sadie?"

"Five. She'll be six in March."

Christa froze. The same age she'd been when her mother died.

For a moment she found herself battling back her own tears. Oh, how she ached for this poor child. At least Christa had still had her father. Sadie lost both of her parents in one fell swoop.

"She's at school right now," Mick added. "Started Monday. She's in kindergarten, so I thought it best we work on getting a routine in place."

"Yes. Definitely. Kids need routine." Didn't mean things were going to be easy, though. For either Sadie or Mick.

"I want to make her feel at home, so I thought I'd surprise her by painting her room."

"Of course, you want her to feel welcome." She looked at the horrid color still in her hand, recalling the wintergreen flavor of the elixir her father had given her every time she had an upset stomach. "But I'm still not going to sell you this color of paint."

"Why not?" He stiffened. "You've seen my place. It's nothing but brown and green. You know, like the outdoors. But Sadie's a little girl, and little girls love pink, don't they?"

"Sometimes. But not necessarily this shade." She held it up so he could get a good look. "Besides, they also like blush, periwinkle and aquamarine."

Shifting from one booted foot to the other, he

ran a hand through his light brown hair. "Oh, boy."

"What is it?" She waved at one of the local contractors as he grabbed two cans of stain from a nearby shelf.

Mick acknowledged the man with a nod before turning back to Christa. "I have no idea what any of those colors are."

Of course he didn't. He was a guy. A man's man, at that. In his world, pink was pink and that's all there was to it.

Moving a few steps toward the paint display, she grabbed swatches of the colors she'd mentioned and set them on the counter in front of him. "Blush, periwinkle and aquamarine." She pointed to each one.

"Looks like pink, purple and blue to me."

She couldn't help the laugh that bubbled out.

The long, tall stretch of cowboy stared down at her, looking more like a brokenhearted little boy. "I can't bring back Sadie's parents, but I want to do everything I can to give her the best life possible. Jen trusted me enough to leave Sadie in my care, and I want to do right by her." The determined edge in his voice was hard to miss.

Christa respected him for that. And while she probably didn't know much more about kids than Mick did, she had once been a little girl and knew what it was like to lose a parent. Enough to nudge her out of her comfort zone and do whatever she could to help Mick create a space little Sadie would love.

"Tell you what. Why don't I drop by this evening with some paint swatches for Sadie to look at? Maybe she and I can talk so I can get a better feel for what she likes. Whether she's into princesses or horses. Then I can help you come up with a plan for her bedroom. Wall color, bedding, pictures—"

He gripped his hat tighter. "You'd do that for me? I mean, you and me don't see eye to eye on a lot of things."

"That's because you're stubborn."

His face turned red. "Well now, ain't that the pot calling the kettle black. Who was it I found stuck up on a ladder last spring, trying to trim some tree branches because she was too stubborn to wait until I could get over there with my pole saw?"

She crossed her arms over her chest. "I am not stubborn." Strong-willed, perhaps. Determined. "Do you want my help or not? I mean, it's obvious you need it." In more ways than one. "You're out of your comfort zone when it comes to decorating for Sadie and, well, I am a girl." She softened her expression. "I'm happy to help." Besides, now that the renovations on her house were complete, she welcomed another challenge. One that would tide her over until she could get her hands on the building next door.

Mick's smile almost erased those lines in his forehead. "I don't know how to thank you, Christa."

"Well, you could start by making sure that brown cow stops moseying into my yard and helping herself to my pansies and purple fountain grass."

He winced. "I don't know why she keeps jumping your cattle guard."

"Isn't it obvious? She likes my flowers."

"I'll see what I can do. Maybe I just need to clean out the cattle guard." He set his hat atop his head. "What time should we expect you to-night?"

"Store closes at five. I should be out of here by five thirty. I'll grab a quick bite to eat and—"

"You could eat with me and Sadie." He shrugged. "Nothing fancy, just some pinto beans and venison sausage, but it'll be hot. And with this cold snap we're having..." He nodded toward the window.

A hot meal waiting for her on a cold winter's night. She could get into that.

"Mind if I bring Dixie?" Since rescuing the two-year-old golden retriever a week before Christmas, Christa had been devoting all of her free time to the dog. She'd never realized how much she'd enjoy having a pet, but Dixie seemed to fill a void, keeping Christa company and giving her a reason to go home at night.

"Are you kidding? Sadie would love having a dog to play with."

"In that case, we'll be there around six."

Watching him retreat, Christa found herself with an admiration for the rugged cowboy that hadn't been there before. He had a tough road ahead of him, navigating the unfamiliar territory of parenthood. Just having a little girl in his house was enough to throw someone like Mick for a loop.

Even though Christa's father had taken care of her since she was born, the role of sole parent had been a challenge. Ballet lessons and playdates had been her mother's forte. Dad wasn't used to fixing dinner every night, nor was he adept at braiding hair. But, like Mick, he bravely faced the challenge before him, determined to fill the gap her mother's death had left behind. And as far as Christa was concerned, she was better because of it.

If Mick raised Sadie with half the passion he approached ranching, hunting and fishing with, then Sadie would thrive. But they had a big adjustment period to get through first. And Christa was happy to help with that in any way she could. Even if it meant spending time with her stubborn neighbor.

Mick Ashford lifted the lid on the cast-iron pot atop the stove in the kitchen of his camp house and gave the beans another stir. He wasn't one to go asking for help, but when Christa offered her assistance with Sadie's room, there was no way he could refuse.

From the moment he'd gotten the call from the authorities three weeks ago, notifying him of his sister's death, his life had been turned upside down. He'd traveled to Colorado to get Sadie, then back to Texas to plan Jen and Kyle's funeral in Fort Worth, all the while having to deal with Kyle's domineering parents and their obvious disdain for both Mick and his sister.

No wonder Kyle had been so adamant about naming Mick as Sadie's guardian in the event anything happened to them. Of course, when Mick agreed, he never imagined it might actually happen. He could only pray that Jen would forgive him for allowing her to be buried in the Sanderson family plot. But between Chuck's badgering, Belita's never-ending tears and the fact that Mick was running on little to no sleep, he'd caved. At least Jen was with Kyle.

Mick replaced the lid, his gaze drifting beyond the Formica-topped island, across the open space to the living area on the opposite side of the room and the little girl with golden-brown hair and green eyes reminiscent of his own. She looked so tiny, sitting in his overstuffed leather recliner while she watched some pony cartoon on the television. Perhaps he should consider getting Sadie her own chair. He could even let her pick it out.

He scrubbed a hand over his face. At this point, he'd do just about anything for his niece. To have her parents stolen from her at such a young age, taken away from everything familiar, then forced to live with a middle-aged cowboy… He'd give her the moon if he could.

A beep sounded from the stove, indicating the oven was hot. Grabbing a pot holder from the counter, he opened the oven door to retrieve the cast-iron skillet inside. He quickly added the corn-bread batter to the hot grease, then returned the pan to the oven and set the timer.

"Uncle Mickey?"

Yeah, he'd even endure being called Mickey. An endearment Sadie had picked up from her mama.

Turning, he saw her little body draped over the arm of the chair. "Yes, ma'am?"

She frowned. "I'm not a ma'am. I'm a girl."

How could he not chuckle? "Okay, then, yes, girl?"

"No." Scowling, she scooted off the chair and marched toward him, still wearing the pink cowboy boots he'd bought her, despite him telling her multiple times that boots were to be left in the mudroom, not worn in the house.

Looking down at her, he said, "All right, princess, what is it?"

Smiling, she held out her arms for him to pick her up and he readily obliged. Sadie sure looked like her mother. And Mick, who'd been ten years old when Jen was born, had been wrapped around his sister's little finger from the day their parents brought her home from the hospital.

After giving him a hug, Sadie met his gaze. "When are we going to eat?"

"Soon. We're just waiting for my friend."

Her little head tilted. "What friend?"

"Miss Christa. She lives in that white house up by the road."

Sadie's eyes widened. "The one with the big tree with the swing?"

"That's the one."

"Do you think she'd let me swing on it?"

"Probably. Once the weather gets a little warmer." He set her feet on the worn vinyl floor he hoped to change out this spring. "Speaking of warmer, I need to stoke that fire." He started toward the woodstove situated in the corner adjacent the couch.

"I'll help." Adding wood to a fire that was inside seemed to be a novelty for Sadie. At least the weather had been cold enough to warrant the stove's use. With Texas winters, you never knew. Eighties one day, thirties the next. Yet this winter had been different, and he was ready for it to be over. He didn't much care for the cold.

A knock sounded at the door, and Sadie immediately changed course and headed in that direction. "She's here!"

"Hold up there, little lady." Fortunately, her miniature legs were no match for his long strides, and he stepped in front of her. "Remember what I said about opening the door?"

"That you *hafta* be with me." Wearing a cheeky grin, she splayed her little arms. "And you're right here."

"Right." Why hadn't he figured that out? "So long as you make sure you adhere to that rule." He reached for the knob, making a mental note that Sadie was much smarter than the average five-year-old. Then again, how would he know? Sadie was the only kid he'd ever been around.

When he opened the door, Sadie gasped. "A doggie!"

Christa smiled, the cold air adding a touch

of pink to her high cheekbones. "You must be Sadie." In one gloved hand she clasped a white gift bag with purple tissue paper poking out the top, while the other held the golden retriever's leash.

"Uh-huh." The kid couldn't seem to take her eyes off the dog.

"I'm Miss Christa." She knelt. "And this is Dixie."

"Hi, Dixie." Sadie finally looked at Christa. "Can I pet her?"

"You sure can. Matter of fact, she loves to be petted."

His niece set one tiny hand atop the dog's furry head.

"I have to warn you, though," said Christa, "she likes to—"

Sadie giggled when the dog licked her chin.

"Give lots of kisses." Christa stood again.

"Y'all come on inside." Mick shivered. "It's freezing out there."

"You'll get no argument from me." The furry pom-pom on Christa's knit hat bounced with each step. "It smells amazing in here." Her compliment had him puffing his chest out a bit.

"Thanks. Dinner's almost ready." He closed the door as she took in the space that encompassed living, kitchen and eating areas. While he liked living in the old camp house he and his father had built when Mick was just a boy, there was nothing feminine about it. From the pine plank walls to the collection of deer trophies lining one wall and the fishing rod rack by the door, this place was the original man cave. Heather, his ex-girlfriend, had hated it. Wanted to make all sorts of changes to the place. Not to mention him.

But for Sadie, he was willing to make a few changes. At least the walls in the upstairs bedrooms were drywalled. He'd sure hate to paint over that pine.

"Well then, since we have a few minutes—" Christa held out the bag "—Sadie, this is for you."

"For me?" The child's eyes went wide, and she managed to tear them away from the dog. "Uncle Mickey, Miss Christa bringed me a present." She accepted the bag and began pulling out the tissue paper.

Removing her gloves and scarf, Christa turned a smirk his way. "Mickey?"

He narrowed his gaze on her. "You're too old to get away with that, so don't even."

"Lookie, look!" Whatever it was, Sadie was excited.

Mick moved closer to see markers in every color of the rainbow and a collection of coloring books. One with a unicorn on the cover, another with horses, and the other two with princesses and mermaids. "That's quite a haul there, kid."

He leaned toward Christa. "I get the feeling you're up to something."

"Don't worry. The markers are washable."

"Good to know." Even if the thought hadn't crossed his mind.

"Which one would you like to color first?" Christa tugged off her hat and shrugged out of her puffy gray coat as she spoke to Sadie.

"Mermaids!"

"Oh, I like that one, too."

The timer on the oven beeped, beckoning him back to the kitchen.

"Does that mean dinner's ready?" Christa called after him.

He pulled the golden-brown corn bread from the oven and set it atop the stove. "Pretty much."

"Good, because I'm hungry." Tucking her wavy, chin-length brown hair behind one ear, she smiled down at Sadie. "How about you?"

"Uh-huh. My tummy growled."

After removing the dog's leash, Christa turned his way. "You need any help, Mick?"

"Uh…sure. Why don't you grab the plates and bowls—" he pointed toward the cupboard next to the stove "—and Sadie, you get the silverware." He'd never had anyone ask him if he needed help before. Then again, up until he returned with Sadie five days ago, it had been just him. Tonight, he had a full house.

Minutes later, they sat at the round, wooden table, Christa across from him, Sadie between them.

"Shall we pray?" Instinctively, he bowed his head.

"Can I do it, Uncle Mickey?"

He popped his head back up, his gaze fixed on Sadie. "Of course you can."

"But we hafta hold hands." She reached one of hers toward Mick and the other toward Christa and they both took hold.

"Okay, we're ready." He watched his niece.

"No, you're not." Sadie scowled at him. "You're 'posta hold Miss Christa's hand."

Christa pressed her lips together, as though she was trying not to laugh.

Shaking his head, he realized that the addition of a child was about to turn his world on end.

He reached across the small table—a move that seemed to sober Christa up. She reluctantly took hold of his hand as Sadie began to pray.

"God is great. God is good."

Christa's hand was soft, her fingers long and slender. Still, that shouldn't make him feel as though sparks were shooting up his arm.

"Let us thank Him for our food. Amen."

He wasn't sure who let go first; all he knew was that neither he nor Christa were interested in holding hands any longer than they had to.

As they neared the end of their meal, Christa said, "Everything was delicious. Especially the sausage. Where did you get it?"

He looked at her across the table. "I made it."

Her eyes went wide. "Wait, you—? How does one make sausage?"

City girl. "It's just venison mixed with a little pork and some seasonings. Then I smoke it in the smokehouse out back. I've got a bunch more in the freezer."

"You have your own smokehouse?" Her expression told him she was impressed. Either that or amused. "I had no idea." She picked up her mason jar of water. "Mick, you are obviously a man of many talents."

Her praise had him clearing the table in an effort to ignore the strange thoughts zinging through his mind. He reached for her plate.

"I can get it, Mick. Let me help you."

"No." The word came out a little gruffer than he'd intended. "You and Sadie need to get your coloring in before bedtime."

Christa's mouth went into the shape of an O. "Bedtime. Yes." Wagging a finger, she continued. "I'd forgotten about that." She turned to Sadie who was chewing her last bite of sausage and petting the dog that had parked itself between Christa and Sadie for the entire meal. "Are you ready to color?"

"Yeah!"

After stoking the fire he'd almost forgotten about, he took care of the dishes, keeping one ear tuned into Christa and Sadie's conversation.

"What color shall we make this mermaid?" Christa dumped the markers on the table while Sadie scrunched her little face up in thought.

"I like this color."

"Aqua is a good color for mermaids."

"'Cept I like this one, too."

Mick craned his neck to see Sadie pointing out the peritwinkle or whatever the color he'd thought was purple actually was.

"Why don't we use them both," Christa suggested. "I bet they'll look really good together."

"Okay!" Sadie took one marker for herself and handed the other to Christa. "I'll color her tail and you can color her hair."

"I hear you have a new bedroom," Christa said as they colored, confirming Mick's suspicion that there'd been a reason for the items Christa brought.

"Uh-huh. My mommy and daddy went to heaven." Despite Sadie's words spilling out as though it was completely normal to have lost her parents, Mick's heart nearly strangled in his chest. "I live with Uncle Mickey now."

Mick swallowed the emotion that lodged in his throat as Christa glanced his way.

Fortunately, her attention quickly shifted back to Sadie. "Want to know a secret?"

Sadie paused her coloring and nodded.

"My mommy went to heaven when I was five."

Mick nearly dropped the soapy plate he was washing. He didn't know Christa had lost her mom when she was little. Why hadn't she mentioned it at the store when he told her about Sadie? Unless it was something she didn't like to talk about. Yet she'd told Sadie.

Cocking her head, his niece studied Christa. "She did?"

"Yes, and I missed her very much."

Sadie scooted out of her chair. "Wanna see my room?" She reached for Christa's hand.

"Sure." Standing, she cast Mick a wary glance. "We'll let Dixie come, too."

As the trio moved up the stairs, Mick suddenly understood why Christa had been so willing to help. And with Sadie slowly but surely realizing that Jen and Kyle were never coming back, help was something he desperately needed. Because he could not, would not disappoint his sister.

Chapter Two

Noting the voice mail from her Realtor the next morning, Christa paused near the paint display at Bliss Hardware, tapped the button and pressed the phone to her ear, hoping for some good news.

"Hi, Christa. Just calling to keep you in the loop. The leasing agent on the Gebhardt building is having problems getting in touch with the owner, so I don't have any news yet. But as soon as I do, you'll be the first to know."

To Christa's surprise, she wasn't disappointed. Then again, the only thing on her radar this morning was Sadie and creating a bedroom that was every bit as special as she was.

Tucking the phone into the back pocket of her jeans, Christa studied the array of paint chips, unable to forget the look on Sadie's face when she had so candidly said that her parents had died. The matter-of-fact revelation was one Christa understood all too well.

When her mother passed away, Christa only had a general idea of what that meant. That her mom wasn't coming home. What her little five-year-old mind couldn't comprehend was that she'd never see her again. She hadn't been prepared for how fiercely she'd miss her mother. What first seemed like an adventure she and her dad had embarked upon soon turned into a heart-wrenching quest to find a new norm. She'd never cried so many tears. Her poor father had done his best to console her, usually to no avail, all the while struggling to come to terms with his own grief.

Locating the right shade for Sadie's room, she grabbed the card, knowing there was no way she could let Mick and Sadie go through this transition without some support. Her support. She had no idea what that might look like, but for now, she would focus on Sadie's room.

The little girl had seemed excited when she showed Christa the corner room last night. It had two windows that would offer lots of natural light, which was good since the space wasn't that big. This light periwinkle would be perfect for the walls. In her online research last night, she'd come across a comforter set that had shades of aqua, fuchsia and yellow that would pop nicely against the walls, without overpowering the room. Then they could add some cute toy bins, hang some pictures…and there had to be a photo of Sadie's parents, perhaps in a pretty frame, someplace where Sadie could easily access it. Christa used to worry she'd forget what her mother looked like. She didn't want Sadie to have those same fears.

Fueled with excitement, she retrieved her phone and typed a text to Mick.

I've got Sadie's room all planned.

And she could hardly wait to get started. Of course, she'd have to show him her ideas first.

She hit Send and started toward the front of the store. The late-morning lull was nearing its end. Things were always busy at lunchtime, with people dropping by to pick up one thing or another while they were on break.

She was about to tuck the phone in her pocket when she felt it vibrate. She looked at the screen to see Mick's response.

Great. Will stop by this afternoon.

Emerging from the narrow paint supply aisle, she pocketed her phone and paused to rearrange the basket of hand pruners and work gloves on the getting-ready-for-spring display as one of her employees hollered.

"It's snowing!"

Christa strolled toward the large windows behind the counter with the cash registers to join her employees in observing the wintry scene. Snow was a rare treat on the coastal plains of Texas and would probably be over in no time.

"You don't s'pose we'll need to close up early, do ya?" Patsy Rodriguez, Christa's assistant manager, came alongside her.

She cast an incredulous look at the sturdy, fifty-year-old redhead. "On account of snow? When was the last time *that* happened?"

"Back when I was in high school." Patsy nodded. "'Course, right about the time things started looking real pretty and white, it turned over to ice."

"I remember that," said Zach Munger, who usually worked out in the store's lumberyard. "I was only in the fourth grade but, as I recall, the whole town pretty much shut down for the better part of a week."

"A week?" Christa couldn't hide her surprise. "That must have been a mighty cold winter."

"Worst I can remember." Patsy shook her head.

"Me, too." Audrey Monroe's long silver hair shimmered under the fluorescent lights as she stared out the window. "Temps dipped way down into the teens and pipes were bursting all over town."

Definitely not the norm for this part of Texas. Still… "I highly doubt there will be a need to close early today. But if there is, we'll cross that bridge when we come to it."

The steady flow of customers between noon and one o'clock was no surprise, though the items they were purchasing were definitely out of the norm. They were snatching up batteries, firewood, flashlights and those foam faucet covers faster than they could restock them, making her wonder if they knew something she didn't.

The white flakes were still coming down when Wes Bishop, a local contractor who was married to Christa's friend Laurel, blew into the store at one thirty.

"Have you got any firewood left?" Wes dusted snow from his dark hair.

"I believe we do." She motioned for him to follow as she made her way toward the back of the store. "Don't tell me you're getting all riled up about this snow, Wes."

"I wasn't. But now they've issued an ice storm warning."

Stopping abruptly, she turned to face him. "When did they do that?" And why wasn't she aware?

"I got the notification on my phone just a little while ago."

She yanked her phone from her pocket and looked at the screen. Sure enough. In effect until noon tomorrow with up to half an inch accumulation of ice. "I had no idea." She turned the ringer on before pocketing the phone.

"According to the radio," Wes continued, "things are going to deteriorate quickly."

"You're kidding?"

"Wish I was. I don't have much firewood at the house. And if the electricity goes out, Laurel, Sarah-Jane and I will be huddled in front of the fireplace."

"Won't we all." Except Christa didn't have a fireplace. Not a working one, anyway.

She continued toward the back of the store and opened the door to discover only half a dozen bundles of wood remained. And while they were decent size bundles… "Looks like this is all I've got, Wes."

"That's okay. It's more than I have right now, so I'll take it all."

On their way to the cash register, her phone beeped. She pulled it out to see a text from Mick.

Change in plans. School canceled. Gotta pick up Sadie.

She looked at Wes. "Apparently they've called off school."

"Good move. Buses and icy roads don't mix."

"Is it icing already?" She moved behind the counter.

"No, but when you're talking about the safety of kids, it's better to be safe than sorry." Wes paid for his wood. "I'll drive around back and load up."

"Sounds good. Stay safe and tell Laurel I said hi."

As Wes left, Christa's phone signaled another text. Mick again.

Better get on home early. Do you need firewood?

Firewood? Not when she didn't have a functional fireplace. When she'd had the chimney cleaned and inspected two years ago, they'd said it had a crack that would need to be repaired before it could be used, so she'd opted to paint the firebox and use it for decorative purposes only. She never imagined she might actually need it for heat.

Her thumbs hovered over the screen a moment before she typed, I don't have a working fireplace. She hit Send before she could think better of it.

Seconds later he responded.

You didn't fix that crack? What if power goes out?

As if that was something she'd even considered a possibility. However, if any of those limbs from the big oak trees she loved so much fell and took down a power line, she and Dixie would be in the dark. Or, more to the point, the cold. And if the roads were icy, the power company might not be able to get to them for days.

Maybe she should go get Dixie and they could stay here at the store. Things probably wouldn't be as bad in town. Except there was no kitchen, only a small microwave. And she'd have to sleep on the floor. Her gaze fell to the old linoleum. Even with the rug in her office, that wouldn't be very comfortable.

Her thumbs moved over the screen.

I'll just have to hope it doesn't.

Hitting Send, she tucked her phone away and headed for her office, determined to ignore any more texts. She was an intelligent woman; surely she could figure something out.

Perhaps she could stay with one of her friends. Maybe Rae or Paisley. They both lived in town. Rae was just around the corn—no, Rae was in Costa Rica on a mission trip. Still, Paisley had a big Victorian house she'd recently started offering as a bed-and-breakfast.

She retrieved her phone again and called Paisley.

"Hi, Christa."

"Hey, Paise. I'm thinking about staying in town tonight. Have you got a room Dixie and I could rent?" Paisley rarely had a full house, and if she did it was only on the weekends or holidays.

"Darlin', you know you wouldn't have to pay for a room here." Yes, she knew, but she wasn't one to take things for granted. "Unfortunately, I don't have a bed to spare."

"You're kidding?"

"I wish I were. That Schmidt boy is getting married this weekend, and the bride's entire family has taken over my house."

"Oh, you poor thing."

"They're not bad. And at least it keeps me busy in the kitchen where it's nice and warm. But if you're in a pinch, you're welcome to bunk with me."

"That's all right. You've got your hands full."

"If you change your mind, just let me know."

"Will do." She ended the call, her gaze traversing the empty store. No point in delaying the inevitable.

Returning to the checkout counter where her

employees continued to gape out the window, she said, "Y'all may as well go on home." She hated the resignation in her voice. And that Patsy was right.

Dwayne Gentry, her right-hand man when it came to knowledge of all things hardware, eased off one of the padded stools behind the counter. "You sure you don't want one of us to stay in case someone needs lumber or something heavy?" Bless the sixtysomething man's heart. He was ever chivalrous.

Patsy shot him a look. "You really think somebody's gonna want lumber in this weather?"

Hands tucked in the pockets of his jeans, the lanky fellow shrugged. "You never know."

"Thank you, Dwayne, but I'll be fine. I'll probably close soon anyway." They'd run out of most of the stuff people wanted.

Once her employees were gone, Christa did a once-over of the store, then parked herself behind the counter, eyeing the darkening sky.

Wait!

She jumped to her feet, remembering the portable propane heaters she carried here at the store. She could use those at home.

Making her way to aisle five, her heart sank as she perused the empty shelves where the heaters had once been. If only she'd thought about them sooner.

The bell rang at the door and she hurried up front as Mick and Sadie blew in, along with a bone-chilling wind that had her pulling her cardigan close.

She couldn't help smiling at the little girl bundled in her fur-hooded coat. "What are you doing here?"

Mick's gaze drove into Christa. "We're here to take you home."

Mick could tell by the fire in Christa's eyes that he'd said that all wrong. "Er, what I meant to say is that we're here to *escort* you home. Things are turning slick fast out there, 'specially on the river bridge." Despite the cold, he found himself sweating. "Since we were already in town…" He lifted a shoulder, knowing he wasn't being totally forthcoming with his neighbor.

She crossed her arms. "So you don't think I'm capable of getting myself home?"

"It's not that. I just figured it wouldn't hurt to have someone watching out for you, that's all."

Christa studied him a moment before turning her attention to his niece. "Sadie, there's a small silver bucket on the table behind the desk in my office—" she pointed toward the room with the door standing open at the far end of the main aisle "—that has candy in it. You're welcome to go grab yourself a couple of pieces if you'd like."

"Yeah!" Sadie looked up at Mick. "Want me to get one for you, too?"

"Sure thing, princess." He winked.

As her boots clomped across the floor, Christa said, "Care to tell me what's really going on?"

He faced her again, knowing she wasn't going to like the full truth any more than the partial truth he'd been trying to get by with. "With them closing the school, I wasn't able to finish puttin' out hay. Something the cows really need when it's cold like this. The calves need it for warmth."

"How warm can it be when it's covered in ice?"

"You'd be surprised. At any rate, I've got one more load I need to haul up the road, but I don't know what to do with Sadie. I mean, it's a closed cab, heated and all, but I just don't know how safe it'd be for her."

"You want me to babysit Sadie?"

He lifted his hat and shoved a hand through his hair before replacing it. "I reckon I do. And I hate to ask. You probably think I'm taking advantage of you because you live so close and all, but I'm in a real pickle."

"Mick, didn't your mama ever teach you that honesty is the best policy?"

"Yes, ma'am. And I wasn't lying. I just wasn't giving you the whole truth."

"You expect me to believe that you would have stopped by here to escort me home even if you didn't need someone to watch Sadie?"

Put like that… "I don't know. Would've depended if I was in town or not."

"Mmm-hmm." She glanced toward her office as Sadie emerged. "I don't mind watching her." Turning, she eyed the window at the front of the store. "Looks like the snow has let up, though."

"No, it's just switching over to ice." He stepped toward the door and opened it to reveal the hissing sound of ice pellets. "Hear that?"

"Yes. Now close the door." Concern filled her hazel eyes and she snugged her sweater tighter. "I guess I should think about getting out of here." She looked at Sadie. "How would you like to hang out with me and Dixie for a little while?"

"I would love that." She looked up at Mick then. "But what about Uncle Mickey?"

"He has to feed the cows."

"Oh." The worry on his niece's precious face had him suddenly concerned. Maybe she didn't want to stay with Christa after all.

He dropped to one knee. "What's wrong, princess? I thought you might want to play with Dixie."

"I do. But—" her eyes filled with tears "—what if you don't come back?"

Mick's heart nearly split in two. He wrapped one arm around Sadie's shoulders and pulled her close, blinking through the moisture that suddenly made it difficult to see. "I won't be gone very long. Just up the road a little way. I've got some calves that need hay to keep them warm." He peered up at Christa, hoping she might have some words of wisdom to offer.

She knelt beside him, taking hold of Sadie's hand. "You can go with your uncle, if you want to."

Those weren't exactly the kind of words he was hoping for.

"But Dixie is going to be sad. Just this morning she was telling me how much she enjoyed meeting you."

With a sniff, Sadie looked at Christa. "Does Dixie have a babysitter?"

"No, she stays by herself when I'm here at work."

"Doesn't she miss you?"

"Yes, she does. When I get home, she runs all over the house like a crazy dog, barking her excitement. Then she drops at my feet and rolls onto her back, expecting me to give her a big ole belly rub."

Sadie giggled. "That's funny."

"You could see for yourself, if you like." Christa pushed to her feet. "You can ride with Uncle Mickey and follow me back to the ranch, then he could drop you off at my house while he goes to feed the cows." She moved behind the counter, retrieved her scarf and slid it around her neck. "Perhaps you could help me figure out what to make for dinner, too." Moving past them and toward her office, she continued. "I don't know about you, but I'm thinking this is perfect soup weather." After disappearing for a brief moment, she emerged, shoving her arms into her coat as she started back toward them. "Or you can go with your uncle to put out hay." She zipped up her coat. "It's up to you."

Whoa. She was good. Mick could only watch in amazement. Christa had laid out Sadie's options, glorifying a few things along the way, trying to nudge her in the right direction, all the while allowing Sadie to choose what she wanted to do instead of telling her what she had to do.

Question was, what would Sadie choose?

After a moment, Sadie grinned. "I want to see Dixie."

Christa perched her hands on her hips. "That is going to make her *so* happy." She looked from Sadie to Mick. "Why don't the two of you wait in the truck while I lock up?"

"Okay." Sadie started for the door without any further discussion.

"I owe you," he whispered to Christa as he turned to follow his niece.

"Oh, you have no idea, cowboy."

He wasn't sure he liked the sound of that. But given the way she'd tempered what could have been an explosive situation, there was no way he could say no.

Chapter Three

Christa couldn't fault Mick for scrambling for a sitter. This storm took a lot of people by surprise, including her. Who knew they'd dismiss school? She was proud of him for dropping whatever it was he'd been doing in order to hurry to town. And taking Sadie on the tractor with him certainly wasn't ideal, even in the best of weather.

She gripped the steering wheel tighter and leaned forward in the driver's seat, eyeing the wet pavement for any ice as the wipers worked in tandem with the defroster to keep her windshield clear. Though she'd never admit it to Mick, she was glad he'd encouraged her to leave when she did, regardless of his motivation. Otherwise, she probably would have hung around the store until five, and there was no telling how bad things would have been by then.

Eyeing Mick's headlights in her rearview mirror, she couldn't help thinking about Sadie's reaction to Mick leaving. Christa understood just how she was feeling. For months after her mother's death, Christa wouldn't let her dad out of her sight, except when she went to school. Looking back, she supposed there was something comforting about being with her friends in a place that was familiar.

But poor Sadie didn't have that. Everything was new for her. Home, school, friends.

Christa fixed her gaze on the road ahead. Sadie's circumstances had stirred more than Christa's compassion, though. They reminded her how alone she was. Christa had lost everyone she'd ever loved. Her mom, her dad… Brody.

Sadie wasn't the only one who was insecure.

Five miles outside of Bliss city limits, she turned from the two-lane county road onto the narrow road that led to her house and promptly hit a patch of ice. Heart pounding, she took her foot off the gas pedal, let go of the steering wheel and shot up another prayer for safety. Her back end shifted slightly, but thanks to the heavy bags of sand Mick had insisted she put in the back of her SUV, she avoided fishtailing.

The next two miles seemed to take forever. A thin layer of snow already coated the less-traveled road. The freezing rain falling now only added insult to injury. Finally, she pulled into her drive and continued under the carport, grateful to have made it safely.

Moments later, Mick's truck eased beside her. Christa exited her SUV, hastily closed the door, then moved to Mick's vehicle to get Sadie.

Reaching for the rear passenger door, she hoped the little girl hadn't changed her mind. Just in case, Christa glanced toward the dining room window that faced the drive and saw Dixie in her usual spot. *Good girl.* And just the ammunition she needed.

She opened the door, pointing toward the house. "Look over there, Sadie. Dixie's waiting for us."

Spotting the dog, her green eyes went wide. "We need to go save her." She unbuckled her seat belt.

"Yes, we do." Christa helped her out of the truck, then looked at Mick.

"I shouldn't be more than an hour," he said.

"Be safe. Dinner will be ready shortly after you get back."

He touched two fingers to the brim of his hat. "I like the sound of that, little lady."

One eyebrow shot up as she closed the door. Little lady? Ha! If her time with Brody Hathaway had taught her anything, it was that she'd never be anyone's little lady. He'd trounced all over her heart and squashed her dreams of a family.

Holding tightly to Sadie's hand, she moved cautiously toward the back porch. As they neared the steps, a gust of wind threatened to knock them over. "Whoa. Hold on, Sadie." They both reached for the railing. "Be extra careful, okay? These steps might be icy."

Sadie moved slowly until they were both safely on the covered porch.

Another blast of wind had the icy rain pelting Christa's cheeks as she fished her keys out of her pocket. When she unlocked the door, a happy Dixie was in the mudroom, waiting to greet them.

"Dixie!" Sadie reached for Dixie's golden mane, but the dog took off into the kitchen, barking, running back and forth through the house, sending area rugs sliding and inadvertently rearranging the wooden chairs around the kitchen table. The child giggled as she watched the crazy dog.

"Hold up there, Dix." Christa opened the door as the dog headed their way again. "You need to go outside."

In a flash, the active pup whisked past them and nearly lost her footing when she bounded down the slippery steps.

Moments later, Dixie raced back up the steps with no more grace than she'd descended.

"Uh-oh. Sadie, you need to mo—" Before Christa could get the words out, Dixie plowed into Sadie, knocking her down.

"Dixie!" Christa tossed the door closed and dropped to her knees. "Shame on you." She shoved the dog out of the way. "Sadie? Honey, are you all right?"

The child rolled onto her back, snickers continuing to bubble out. Thankfully, she was still bundled in her coat. All that padding probably protected her.

Christa pulled Sadie to her feet and urged her into the kitchen before shoving her hood back to reveal flyaway golden-brown hair and pink cheeks. "Please tell me you're not hurt."

"No." Breathy titters still came from the child as she looked up at her. "That was fun."

Unzipping her own coat, Christa said, "Well, I'm glad you enjoyed it." She, on the other hand, was worn out.

Sadie clumsily removed her coat, shoving her hair out of her face. "What are we going to do now?"

Christa reached around the corner to hang their coats on hooks in the mudroom. "First, we're going to wash all the dog slobber off your face, then I have to start fixing dinner. You can

either help me or you can play with Dixie—
please don't let her lick you—or you can tell
me what you'd like to do."

Once Sadie was cleaned up, she opted to play
ball with the dog while Christa set to work on
the chicken soup she'd been contemplating for
two days. Once the meat and veggies were on
to simmer, she turned to find Dixie lying on her
back next to the kitchen table while Sadie happily rubbed her belly.

"Dixie loves belly rubs."

"That's why she's smiling."

Cocking her head, Christa peered down at
the goofy dog. "Yep, she sure is." She turned
her attention back to Sadie. "I have some dough
in the refrigerator. Would you like to help me
make cookies?"

"Oh, yes, please." She bolted to her feet. "I
love making cookies. Not as much as I like eating them, though."

"Well, then we may be cut from the same
cloth."

Sadie cocked her head. "What does that
mean?"

"It means we're alike."

Christa retrieved the tube of chocolate chip
cookie dough.

"Those are the same kind of cookies I used
to make with my mommy."

Christa's steps slowed. Had she just turned what could have been a happy moment into one filled with sorrow? Then she recalled making cookies with her own mother.

Grabbing the step stool from beside the fridge, she placed it in front of the counter to the right of the stove. "You can stand on this." While Sadie complied, Christa retrieved cookie sheets from the cupboard. "I used to make cookies with my mom, too. Except her dough came from a bowl, not a tube."

"We really are from the same cloth." Elbow resting atop the concrete countertop, Sadie looked contemplative. "Our mommies both died and we bakeded cookies with them." She smiled then, as though she'd just realized the same thing Christa had. That, perhaps, God had brought the two of them together for a reason.

When the cookies came out of the oven, both Sadie and Christa sampled the fruits of their labor. Okay, so there hadn't been much laboring, but they still deserved a treat.

Midway through a game of Go Fish with Sadie, Christa eyed the antique schoolhouse clock that ticktocked on the kitchen's far wall. Mick would be back anytime. After being out in the cold, he'd be more than ready for something hot, so she turned up the heat a notch on the simmering soup and added the noodles.

Thirty minutes later, dinner was ready. Fifteen more passed and there was still no sign of Mick. Not the first thing that hadn't gone according to plan today, she reminded herself. But after a second loss to Sadie, another round of cookies and the incessant sound of ice pelting the window, Christa began to worry.

While Sadie played on the rug in the living room with a set of vintage Lincoln Logs Christa had picked up at a flea market, Christa stole a few surreptitious glances out the window, hoping to see the lights of Mick's tractor. Instead, there was only darkness.

What was taking him so long? He said an hour. Two had passed. He had her number. He would have called or texted if there was a problem. Right?

A feeling of dread threatened to overtake her, but she refused to give in. Mick was fine. The weather must have caused things to take longer than usual, that was all. And if she called him, it would only delay him further.

A gust of wind rattled the windows on the old house.

Glancing over her shoulder, she saw that Sadie was oblivious.

"What are you building?" Pulling her cardigan around her, Christa moved to the sofa and plopped down.

"A doghouse for Dixie."

Christa eyed the miniature structure. "I don't think she'll fit in that."

"I know. But we could build a big one that looks just like it."

A thud on the back porch had Christa standing. She'd just started into the kitchen when she heard something akin to a knock coming from the door. Her steps quickened as she hurried into the mudroom. Shoving the curtain aside, she saw an ice-coated Mick.

She jerked the door open. His coat and insulated overalls were covered in a layer of white while miniature icicles hung from the brim of his hat and his face was beet red. Without thinking, she reached for his arm and pulled him inside. "What happened?"

"B-battery died on the tractor. Had to w-walk b-back."

"In this weather? Why didn't you call me?"

"My ph-phone was dead, too."

"Oh, Mick." She helped him out of his coat then urged him into the kitchen as Sadie bounded in with Dixie at her side.

"You look like a snowman, Uncle Mickey."

"Yeah, I feel like one, too, princess." He pulled a chair away from the table and dropped into it. He looked exhausted.

Christa emptied the pockets of his coat. "I'm

going to put this in the dryer and get you a blanket." Momentarily setting the coat aside, she hastily grabbed a handled bowl from the cupboard, filled it with soup and set it beside him. "Be careful, this is really hot." She grabbed a spoon from the drawer. "But at least it'll warm you up."

"Smells good."

"It is good." Scooping up the coat, she returned to the mudroom as another wind gust shook the house. A moment later, everything went black.

The only thing Mick could make out in the darkened kitchen was the flame under the pot on the stove.

"Uncle Mickey?" A tremor laced Sadie's voice.

"I'm right here, princess." He reached in the direction she'd been standing when the power went out.

She quickly latched on to his arm before crawling into his lap, her warmth as welcome as a rain shower in a drought.

Seemed he couldn't catch a break today. First the weather, then school letting out early, a broken-down tractor, having to trek two miles through the wind and ice, and now, before he'd even had a chance to thaw out, the power was gone. And to think folks in other parts of the country spent months with weather like this. Not him. He hated the cold, which was why he lived in Texas. God was proving He had a sense of humor today, though.

"Well, that was bad timing." Christa aimed the flashlight on her phone in his direction. "Now I can't dry your coat."

"At least we've got hot soup." He nodded to the bowl she'd given him.

"Stand by." Her light retreated into the mudroom then reappeared, growing brighter as she drew closer to the table. "I knew this stash of flashlights would come in handy someday." She clicked one on and handed it to Sadie.

"Oh, thank you." She danced the beam across the ceiling.

Turning on the other two, Christa stood them on the table, their beams aimed upward, affording them some much-needed light. "There. Now we don't have to eat in the dark." Her gaze moved to Sadie. "You ready for some soup?"

"Yes, please." She shone the beam on Christa's dog. "Look, Dixie. I got my own flashlight."

Suddenly the darkness had turned into an adventure for Sadie. No telling how long it'd be before the power came back on. And that created a major dilemma. One he wasn't ready to bring up just yet. Not when he felt completely wrung out.

Reaching to his left, he pulled out the chair beside him. "Sadie, why don't you sit here next to me while we eat our soup?"

"Okay."

Christa approached, carrying two more bowls with handles. "Here you go, Sadie." She set the first bowl in front of his niece before sitting across from him with her own.

After a quick prayer, Mick wrapped one bone-chilled hand around the bowl while the other ladled a spoonful of the steaming broth into his mouth. "Mmm, this is good." He grabbed a second spoonful. "And not just because it's hot."

"If the heat's not enough to warm you up, the garlic and red pepper flakes should."

"That's what I'm tasting. I wondered what that kick was." It felt good going down.

"We have cookies, too." A noodle dangled from Sadie's bottom lip. "Miss Christa letted me help."

"I'm sure they're delicious then." He took another spoonful. "I think I'll need a second helping of soup before I have a cookie, though."

Things fell silent then. But as Christa finished her soup, she said, "So what do we do about the electricity?"

"You can call in the outage," he said. "Don't

know how long it'll take 'em to get on it. Maybe not until the storm passes. Even then, depends how many folks are without power."

"You don't think they'll get to it tonight?" That was a crazy question. She'd lived in Bliss long enough to know things out here operated at a different pace than in the city.

"Wouldn't count on it."

"But it'll be freezing in here. What am I supposed to do without any heat? Light my oven and sleep in the kitchen?"

"Wouldn't recommend it."

Even with the dim lighting, he could see her glaring at him from across the table. "Then what would you advise? And yes, I know that if I'd gotten my fireplace fixed we wouldn't be having this conversation."

"You brought that up, not me." He scooped up the last piece of carrot and a chunk of chicken.

"Oh, like you weren't thinking it."

"No, I wasn't." He grabbed a napkin from the holder on the table. "What I was thinking, though, is that we're going to need to head down to the camp house pretty soon. I stoked the fire before I headed out on the tractor, but I don't want to let it get too low." Not that he relished the thought of going back out in that cold.

"Do you think you have electricity at your place?"

"No. I mean it's possible, just not probable. Depends if the problem is here at your place or somewhere else. Since I didn't hear anything that sounded like a limb falling, I'm guessing it's somewhere up the line. But you should still notify them that you're in the dark."

"But if your electric is out, too, why do I need to go to your place?"

"Because I've got a woodstove for heat. Downstairs anyway. Which means you two will be camping in the living room."

"I like camping." Sadie grinned. "Can Dixie sleep by me?"

Christa looked more than a little chagrined. "Why didn't I grab one of those indoor propane heaters we carry at the store?"

"Probably would have been a good idea." Bowl in hand, he stood and crossed to the stove for a refill.

"By the time I thought about it, we were sold out." Leaning back in her chair, she blew out a breath as he sat back down. "Only had two to begin with."

"You oughta start making a list of all the things you wish you'd done and then go ahead and do them once this storm is over, so you'll be prepared next time."

"You mean in another twenty years." She crossed her arms over her chest.

"At least you'll be prepared."

"You sound like my father. He always said the best time to prepare for an emergency is before there's an emergency."

"Smart man."

"He was." She stared at her empty bowl. "He passed away four years ago." Standing, she grabbed her dishes and moved to the sink. Turned on the water. Or tried to anyway. "Oh, come on. Now I don't have any water?"

"Your water runs on a pump and when there's no power to the pump—"

"All right, I get the picture." She released a sigh before addressing him again. "So, what's the plan?"

"For starters, why don't you go gather your things. I'd recommend clothes you can layer, some heavy sweaters, if you have any."

"How long do you think I'll have to stay with you?"

"That's going to depend on the weather and you."

"Me?"

"Yeah, 'cause I'm pretty sure that if you get mad enough, you're going head back up whether there's power or not."

"Funny, Ashford. Beyond clothes, what should I bring?"

"Got any bottled water?"

"I always keep two cases on hand."

"Good. Bring it."

"What about food? You have a gas stove, right?"

"Yes, and they just filled my propane tank so we can cook up a storm."

"Bad choice of words."

"By the way, we'll need to take your vehicle down to my place. I went out on the tractor, so my truck is at the house."

When Christa finished gathering her clothes, a couple of blankets and a comforter, she and Sadie proceeded to comb the kitchen with their flashlights, gathering food items, while he warmed up Christa's SUV and began loading.

The wind swirled around him, ice pelting his face. Hard to believe this all started with some pretty snow.

He'd just set Christa's suitcase in the cargo area when he saw headlights coming up the road. "I'd hate to be that person." He was about to close the hatch when he realized it was a sheriff's vehicle. But why was it pulling into his and Christa's drive?

Mick waved as the headlights illuminated the space around him. Maybe they were just covering the area, looking for stranded cars and happened to see him. Since he knew most everyone on the force, they might just want to make sure everything was all right.

The Chevy Tahoe came to a stop beside him and, a moment later, the door opened.

Mick recognized his old classmate Rhett Connors right away.

Using his gloved hand to shield his face from the icy onslaught, he said, "Hey, Rhett. How's it going?"

"Well as can be expected."

Mick turned up the collar on his coat as the deputy drew closer. "How are the roads holding up?"

"Gettin' worse by the minute." Keeping one hand on his Stetson to prevent it from blowing off his head, Rhett scanned the sky. "Sure wish I didn't have to be out in this mess."

"Well, so far so good out here." Mick poked a thumb toward the house. "Christa's power's out and her fireplace is out of commission, so my niece and I are helpin' her pack up so we can head down to my place. I've got plenty of wood, so we should be able to ride things out just fine."

"That's good to know." The man lowered his gaze, leveling it on Mick. "I hate to tell you this, Mick, but I'm here on official business."

"Business? In this weather?"

Rhett reached inside his heavy coat, pulled out an envelope and handed it to Mick. "Sorry, but someone's filed a lawsuit against you. You've been served."

Chapter Four

An hour and a half after the power had gone out, Christa stood in front of the wood-burning stove in Mick's living room, grateful to have heat again, and curious as to what was bothering the rugged cowboy. A scowl marred his handsome features on the short ride to his house, and he'd seemed annoyed as he added more wood to the fire.

She shouldn't be so hard on him, though. If she'd been forced to walk even a short distance in this weather, she'd be out of sorts, too. But given that he was already frozen to the bone, why had he been talking to that sheriff's deputy for so long? A welfare check was one thing, but chitchatting in the midst of an ice storm was just plain dumb.

Blowing out a breath, she tried not to take his foul mood personally. Mick probably wasn't any happier about this turn of events than she was. Which would explain his eagerness to go out to his truck to charge his phone once they'd unloaded her SUV.

In the dim light provided by the fire and a battery-operated lantern that had been positioned on the kitchen island separating the cooking and living spaces, Christa's gaze drifted to the couch where Sadie lay on one end. Still wearing her coat and boots, she had one arm draped over the side so she could pet Dixie on the floor beside her. Evidently the cold didn't bother them, while Christa couldn't seem to get warm.

Though they'd been without power at her place for only an hour or so, it didn't take long for the temperature to drop inside. That's what she got for deciding against new, energy-efficient windows. But no matter how hard she tried, no matter how logical it seemed, she couldn't bring herself to let go of those old windows. The variations and bubbles in the glass held a charm that simply couldn't be replaced.

As Sadie's eyelids began to droop, Christa checked her watch, surprised to discover that it was almost nine. She scanned the area around her. With only the sofa and a recliner, their sleeping options were fairly limited. Though, perhaps she and Mick could bring down the twin mattress from Sadie's room once he returned.

The door opened then, and Mick slipped inside, quickly shutting it behind him. "I need some coffee." His voice was gruff, and he continued into the kitchen without so much as glancing her way.

"How?" She started toward him. "No power means no coffee maker."

"I'll improvise, all right?"

Christa stopped in her tracks. Either the cold or exhaustion had gotten to him, because in the three years she'd known him, she'd never heard Mick use a sharp tone like that. With her boots riveted to the vinyl floor, she continued to watch him. Even in the low light she could see the exaggerated rise and fall of his shoulders.

He turned. "I'm sorry. I shouldn't have snapped like that." Then he went back to his mission, pouring water from a gallon jug into a saucepan.

Christa tiptoed to the couch to check on Sadie. Despite Mick's sharp words, she was sound asleep.

With a fortifying breath, Christa joined Mick in the kitchen. "Hey." She set a hand on his back.

He looked down at her, his green eyes filled with an ache that made her heart go out to him.

He'd been trying so hard to take care of Sadie, his cattle, even Christa, yet the cold had all but sucked the life right out of him.

"Sadie's asleep," she said. "Do you want to leave her on the sofa?"

Using a long-tipped multipurpose lighter, he ignited the gas burner beneath the saucepan. "The couch folds out into a bed." His voice was softer now. "You and Sadie can sleep there, or you can take the recliner."

"Where are you going to sleep?"

"In my bedroom."

"Upstairs? It'll be freezing up there."

"I've got a subzero rated sleeping bag. Besides, I like to sleep in my own bed."

Christa knew good and well he'd be sleeping in the living room if she wasn't here. Yet even after all he'd been through tonight, he was forgoing a warm space for her. His gallantry warmed her almost more than the stove.

She hated to add more to his already overflowing plate, but better to get things done now so he could relax. "Would you mind taking care of the bed while I get Sadie ready?"

"No, this water's gotta heat anyway."

Christa scooped up the sleeping child and moved to the recliner to take off her coat and boots while Mick pulled out the bed and added sheets, pillows and the down comforter and blanket Christa had brought.

Once the bed was ready, she settled Sadie beneath the covers before joining Mick in the kitchen. After ditching his coat, he'd prepared the coffee maker as usual, except he was pouring the hot water from the saucepan into the filter a little at a time.

"Smart idea." She moved alongside him, noting the battle-weary look on his face. "You've had a rough day."

"I'm a rancher. I can handle rough." He added the last of the water and watched it drip into the carafe as the aroma of coffee wafted around them. "But that deputy didn't stop by just to be friendly. He was here on business."

Business? But Mick was still standing here and hadn't been arrested. "I don't understand."

"He served me with papers."

"For what?"

He glanced toward the couch then cleared his throat. "Sadie's grandparents, Kyle's parents, want custody of Sadie. They're claiming I'm unfit to raise her."

Fiery heat prickled through Christa as her blood began to boil. "You've been nothing but wonderful with Sadie."

"But I'm a single guy."

"So was my dad." Her hands fisted, what little nails she had digging into her palms. "And he raised me just fine."

A hint of a smile tugged at his lips. "You might want to keep your voice down, so you don't wake Sadie."

She slipped off her coat and tossed it over the back of a chair. "Needless to say, I have a very strong opinion on this."

"You don't say?" He picked up the carafe. "Why don't I explain things over coffee."

He poured two cups then joined her at the table. "I'm pretty sure Kyle's parents are upset because they thought they were going to be raising Sadie. You should have seen the looks on their faces when they learned Jen and Kyle had appointed me as Sadie's guardian."

She clutched the cup in her hands, savoring its warmth. "I'm impressed they had the forethought to do that. Most people don't even consider that sort of stuff."

Still wearing his insulated overalls, he wrapped his calloused fingers around the oversize mug. "Kyle was adamant because he didn't want his folks to have any influence over Sadie's life."

"But they're her grandparents." She blew on the steaming liquid. "Did he have a falling out with them or something?"

Mick took a swig before setting his mug back

on the table. "Do the names Chuck and Belita Sanderson ring any bells?"

"Yes." She thought for a moment. "Isn't he some big wig in the energy industry? Served in Congress or something?"

"Yep. And they're one of the wealthiest families in Texas."

"So, they could certainly provide for Sadie financially."

Swallowing another sip of the strong brew, Mick shook his head. "Kyle wasn't worried about that. He had plenty of his own money. Money that now belongs to Sadie. I don't plan to touch it, except maybe for her college." He stared at the flames flickering behind the glass on the other side of the room. "Kyle was an only child. And growing up, he always had nannies and such, until he was old enough for his parents to send him off to a private school." Facing her again, he continued. "He hardly ever saw his parents unless it was convenient for them. Kyle said he promised himself that if he ever had children, they would know they were important and that he loved them and wanted to be with them."

"Can't say that I blame him. I mean, why even bother having a child if you don't want them around?" She took her first sip.

"To have somebody to take over the family business, carry on the family name."

"That's rather archaic."

"Not when you're a billionaire, I guess." He lifted his cup. "Kyle had the paperwork drawn up the day after Sadie was born."

"I guess that shows just how adamant he was. Not to mention how much he loved his daughter."

Mick's countenance fell once again as he stared into his cup. "I don't know what I'm going to do, Christa. The Sandersons are used to getting their way. I wouldn't put anything past them."

Unable to stop herself, she reached for him, and instantly regretted it. His hand was warm, his grip almost desperate as it swallowed hers, infusing her with a determination to do anything and everything to see that Sadie remained in his care.

Trying to avoid those green eyes that seemed to be pleading with her to make things right, she said, "The first thing you need to do is talk to your attorney. Although that means waiting and I know that's something you probably don't want to do. I don't either. So for now, I guess we'll do the only thing we can."

"What's that?"

She dared to meet his gaze. "Pray."

* * *

Hints of daylight peered through the blinds as Mick made his way downstairs the next morning, in need of coffee. While he'd managed to stay warm enough during the night, sleep was evasive. He felt as though he'd been caught in a stampede. His body ached from trekking through the ice and wind while his mind had been under assault with a glut of what-ifs.

With Christa and Sadie still asleep, he tiptoed into the kitchen in his sock feet and quietly added water to the saucepan he'd used last night. He'd need to talk to his lawyer ASAP, because he would not let Jen and Kyle down. Yet no matter how tightly he clung to that, he couldn't help wondering what would happen if a judge decided Sadie would be better off with her grandparents. Granted, they'd only been together for three weeks, yet Mick couldn't imagine life without her. She'd been a breath of fresh air in his otherwise mundane existence.

This wasn't about him, though. He set the pan atop the stove, twisted the knob and ignited the burner with a lighter. If Sadie wanted to be with her grandparents, he'd have no choice but to let her go. However, given the way she'd pulled away from both Chuck and Belita whenever they decided to pay her any mind, Mick doubted that would happen. She barely knew them. Still, what if she was forced to live with the Sandersons?

"It's morning!"

Sadie's proclamation had Mick eyeing the sofa sleeper across the room. "Mornin', princess."

She was sitting up, her hair going this way and that, her smile as big as ever. At least she'd slept well.

Beside her, a comforter-covered Christa groaned, momentarily silencing his torment. He was thankful she'd been here last night. Without her to talk to, he might have gone out of his mind. There weren't many people in Mick's life he could confide in. Just Jen and Bum, an older rancher who lived down the road and had become a mentor after Mick's father passed eighteen years ago. Now Jen was gone.

He swallowed the sudden lump in his throat. Having Christa on his side meant a lot.

Her dog popped up from the floor then and promptly licked her face.

"Really, Dix." Christa pulled the covers over her head.

"Dixie!" Sadie cheered.

"Don't encourage her, Sadie." Christa's voice was muffled.

"But she likes to give kisses." Sadie climbed over Christa to pet the dog.

"She's probably ready to go outside, too." Christa dragged herself upright, her hazel eyes colliding with Mick's. "What does it look like out there?"

"Don't ask me, I just woke up, too. But as of a couple of hours ago, it was still coming down."

"And how would you know that?" She yawned.

"Somebody had to make sure the fire kept going. Speaking of that." Still wearing his jeans and Henley from yesterday, he started toward the woodstove.

"Couldn't shut down your brain, could you?" Tossing the covers aside, Christa swung her legs over the side of the bed.

"Nope." The aroma of burning wood drifted into the space as he opened the door on the stove. He grabbed three logs from the dwindling stack beneath the window, glad he had plenty more on the porch.

"Me either." Christa stood and stretched, looking far too cute in sweatpants, a big, bulky sweater and fuzzy socks.

"By the way, I got an alert on my phone around four that schools are closed." He latched the door on the stove.

"As if there was any doubt." Rubbing the dog's head, she sent Mick a sleepy smile. "Thank you for allowing me and Dixie to stay here."

"I couldn't very well leave you with no heat."

"This coming from the guy who slept in a room with *no* heat."

"Ah, I was warm enough. Heat rises, remember?" He pointed toward the ceiling. "My room is right up there." It was a thousand other things that had prevented him from sleeping.

The canine that always seemed to be smiling trotted toward the door.

Christa followed, let her outside, then stared out the window. "I don't know if it's snow or sleet, but something is still falling from the sky. It sure is pretty."

"I want to see." Sadie bounded off the bed.

Mick intercepted her, scooping her into his arms before joining Christa.

"Oh…" The wonder that filled Sadie's green eyes when she took in the wintry scene warmed his heart, steeling his determination to make sure she remained in his care.

Turning his attention outside, he couldn't help but smile. Beneath a canopy of thick, gray clouds, a layer of white spread over the ground like frosting on a cake. Midway between the house and the cow pond that doubled as his favorite fishing hole, the big live oak dripped with icy leaves, while loblolly pine branches bowed under the weight of their sparkling needles at the water's edge.

"Amazing how a little ice can transform a dull, dormant landscape into something so pretty." He looked at Christa. "However, I sure am glad we put our vehicles under my carport."

"No kidding. It would take forever to get all that ice off the windshields. And I'm planning to head into town later this morning to check on the store. You know, after it's had a chance to warm up some."

"To a balmy twenty-eight degrees?"

Looking up at him, she said, "I thought it was supposed to get above freezing today."

"Not according to this." Removing his phone from his pocket, he pulled up the weather forecast and showed it to her.

"That says tomorrow's high is only thirty-four."

"Last time I checked, that's above freezing."

She sent him an indignant glare.

"Don't look at me. I had nothing to do with it."

Dixie rejoined them, so he let Sadie down to play with her before heading to the kitchen to make the coffee.

"All I know is that I'm going to have to make sure Sadie is bundled up good when we head out." He swapped out the filter from last night and added a couple scoops of coffee.

"Head out where?" Christa followed him. "To play?"

"No, to fix the tractor." He poured the boiling water over the filter a little bit at a time. "Cows are going to need more hay, so I have to change out that battery. Good thing I have a new one in the barn." He just wished he'd have taken care of it sooner and saved himself a lot of trouble.

She glanced over her shoulder to check on Sadie. When she turned back, she lowered her voice. "What are you thinking? You can't make Sadie walk two miles in this weather."

"I know that. We'll take the utility vehicle. Course I'll have to leave it in the pasture until I can retrieve it later, but the tractor cab is heated."

Steam rose from the coffeepot, filling the room with its inviting aroma.

"I can't believe you're considering having her go with you to put out hay."

He emptied the pan and set it aside. "What else am I supposed to do? Ranchers don't get bad-weather days. My cattle are my livelihood and they need more hay. I can't ignore them any more than you can ignore your store. Sure, it's not ideal, but Sadie lives with me now, so I'm just going to have to find a way to make it wor— What's that?"

A rumbling noise filtered in from outside.

"I don't know." Christa looked at him.

"Sounds like a tractor." He hastily headed for the door. "I'll be right back." He shoved his feet into his boots. "Sadie, you stay inside with Christa." He yanked his coat from the back of one of the dining chairs and put it on as he headed outside.

The subfreezing air slapped him in the face and sent a chill through him. Zipping up his coat, he stepped off the porch as Bum's big blue tractor approached.

The man who had been his father's best friend eased it to a stop and set the brake before opening the door and climbing down from the cab. His standard cowboy hat had been replaced with a red-and-black-checked, fur-lined trapper hat that made Mick chuckle.

"What're you laughing at?" Bum's smile made his silver-blue eyes sparkle as he shoved his gloved hands into the pockets of his insulated coveralls.

"Nice hat."

"Hey, don't go pokin' fun, boy." He carefully picked his way over the icy terrain. "Dorothy got this for me. Keeps this bald head of mine nice and warm." Dorothy had passed away last year, just shy of her and Bum's fiftieth wedding anniversary.

"If you say so." Mick nodded toward the

house. "Come on in and say hi to Sadie and Christa."

"Christa's here?" Bum looked more than a little surprised.

"Her fireplace isn't in working condition, so I couldn't very well let her freeze." He lifted a shoulder. "Besides, Sadie likes playing with Dixie."

Reaching the porch, they stomped the ice from their boots.

"What are you doing over here anyway?" Mick reached for the door.

"Headin' to your hay barn."

"What for?" Mick paused. "You run out of hay?"

"No, but that's for my cows. I'm here to feed yours. Saw your tractor over in the east pasture." The older man poked a thumb over his shoulder. "When you weren't in it, I figured there was a problem."

"You got that right." He opened the door, explaining what had happened.

Inside, the aroma of fresh-brewed coffee mingled with a hint of smoke.

"We've got company," he said.

"Hi, Bum." Christa smiled, her hands wrapped tightly around a steaming mug.

Out of the corner of his eye, Mick saw a curious Sadie bounding toward him. He picked her up. "Sadie, this is my friend, Mr. Bum."

"It's a pleasure to meet you, Sadie." Bum removed his hat. "I've heard a lot about you."

She smiled shyly.

Smoothing a hand over her back, Mick said, "I've known Mr. Bum since I was littler than you."

Her green eyes moved from Bum to Mick and back. "Did you know my mommy?"

If the comment surprised Bum, he didn't let on. "I sure did, sweetheart. And you look just like she did at your age."

Christa approached. "Care for a cup of coffee, Bum?"

"No, thank you, young lady. I just wanted to make sure y'all were doin' all right."

"So far, so good." She shrugged. "How are the roads?"

"Empty. Except for some old codger in a big ole tractor." He winked.

She laughed. "Well, I was hoping to run into town later."

Bum shook his head. "I wouldn't advise it. Least not today. Too dangerous."

"Oh." Christa's shoulders dropped a notch.

"Hopefully, they'll get our power back on tomorrow." The older man settled his hat back on his head. "Tractor's running so I'd better get on."

Mick put Sadie down and followed the man.

"You be careful out there, Bum!" Christa hollered after them.

"Will do."

Approaching the tractor, Mick said, "You don't need to worry about my cattle. I've got things covered." Or would, just as soon as he swapped out that battery.

"No, you don't, Mick." Bum faced him now. "You will eventually, but right now, you've got your hands full. Though it appears you've got some mighty fine help." He winked.

Mick wanted to argue, but he couldn't. Hard to believe that until two days ago, he and Christa only saw each other in passing here at the ranch, at church or if he happened into the hardware store. Sure, there'd been a couple of times when he'd helped her with outdoor projects like trimming limbs and getting her mower started for her, but for the most part, they ran in different circles. Yet the past thirty-six hours, they'd been almost joined at the hip. All because of Sadie. Christa not only cared about his niece, she could relate to her in a way Mick couldn't.

"God's given you a great gift in the form of that little girl. Enjoy your time with her today." Bum peered up at the sky. "Storms like this don't come along but once or twice in a life-time. Make it a memorable event for her." He started up the steps on the tractor. "Besides, I need something to do. I'll go stir-crazy cooped up in that house alone."

Mick's heart went out to the man. While Mick was used to being alone, it was all new to Bum. "Well, if you want some company, my door's always open."

The older man smiled. "I 'preciate that, son. And I'm here if you need me."

Perhaps that was part of Mick's problem. He wasn't used to needing anyone. Yet suddenly, he found himself more needy than ever. So, while he would accept Bum's and Christa's help, he had to find a way to juggle ranching and Sadie. Otherwise, it could cost him the greatest gift he'd ever been given.

Chapter Five

"Tell me what's going on in town." Taking full advantage of the hands-free feature in her idling SUV, Christa nestled into her heated seat Friday afternoon, eager to know what was happening in Bliss proper. "Have you been out at all, Patsy? What shape are the streets in? Have you been to the hardware store?"

"Whoa. Slow down there, boss. I can't get a word in edgewise."

"Sorry." Christa felt so cut off, though. The hardware store was her baby, and she'd never been away from it this long.

"I wandered up to the store earlier today and everything is fine," Patsy continued. "A few folks were out looking around, taking pictures, but nobody's driving anywhere. Not with all this ice. Besides, the town is pretty much shut down so there's nowhere to go *to*."

"What about power?"

"Some people have it, some don't. I heard they opened the elementary school as a warming center in case folks are hurtin'."

"Was it on at the store?"

"Yes, ma'am."

Great. She should have stayed there.

"All right, Patsy, I guess we'll talk in the morning."

The precipitation had finally come to an end late yesterday, though temps were still below freezing. Perhaps now that the clouds were breaking, things would warm up.

A sense of relief settled over Christa. With everyone else stuck at home, she didn't have to worry about losing customers. Still, she wanted Bliss Hardware to be open once they were able to get out and about. Being part of the community meant being able to meet her customers' needs.

Leaning her head against the seat back, she studied the row of icicles hanging from the edges of Mick's metal roof. Once the sun came out, maybe things would get back to normal. Though she had to admit, yesterday had been fun.

After Mick talked with his attorney and Bum took him over to replace the battery in his tractor, he, Christa and Sadie took the opportunity to enjoy some things they normally wouldn't have had time for. Like exploring the wintry countryside, drinking hot chocolate while playing board games and baking sugar cookies from scratch. With just the three of them, it had been a bit like playing house. Except Christa was too old and jaded for pretend.

She hadn't always been that way, though. Once upon a time, she'd envisioned being married and having a couple of kids. Then she went off to college and those thoughts faded into oblivion as she became increasingly focused on her career. The next thing she knew, she was hopping from one start-up tech company to another, constantly challenging herself to do bigger and better things. Innovation, creation and growth were her forte.

Then she met Brody, and he was every bit as driven as she was. They worked on projects together, shared ideas and even talked about starting their own company. No one had ever understood her drive the way Brody had and, before long, those dreams of a family sparked to life once again. She'd trusted Brody with her heart, her dreams and so much more.

When he surprised her with dinner at one of Austin's finest restaurants, she just knew he was going to propose. Instead, he told her he'd taken a job in Atlanta. Said he'd been looking for months. The worst part was when she asked where that left them and he informed her there was no them. That he'd enjoyed their time together, but she wasn't relationship material.

She'd been duped. Used. Heartbroken.

Shoving the morose thoughts aside, she unplugged her phone from the charger and turned off the ignition. It was time to return to reality. Just as soon as the power came back on.

Mick met her at the door as she made her way onto the porch. "Good news."

"Oh?"

"Power's back on."

Her insides tangled as sorrow somehow squelched her happiness. Was he eager to get rid of her? Not that she should care. She was ready to get back to her place and for life to return to normal. Lonely and normal. At least she had Dixie to keep her company.

"That's great." Moving past him, she savored the comforting aroma of burning wood that told her he'd probably just stoked the fire. "I guess I'll gather my things and head back home."

"Now, hold on." He followed her, closing the door behind him. "Don't go gettin' ahead of yourself. I think we should all drive up there first to make sure everything is in order."

She supposed that was a good idea. She'd hate

to gather up everything only to discover that her power was still out.

"Well, my car is all warmed up, so we may as well take it."

Fifteen minutes later, she eased her SUV to a stop just short of her own carport and simply stared. She'd never seen her two-story farmhouse look this way before—as though it belonged in a Christmas movie. The white house with dark green shutters smack-dab in the middle of a sea of white. The only thing missing was a mass of twinkling lights.

"I've got to get a picture of this." She snatched her phone from the console. "Y'all stay put. I'll be right back." She followed her tire tracks back to the drive, not wanting to mar the pristine scene with any footprints, then continued to the road.

White coated the roof and icicles graced the edges of both the main roof as well as the one over the porch. Only then did she realize she'd failed to remove the faux evergreen wreath from her front door.

"Perfect."

A few shots later, she returned to Mick and Sadie. "We can go inside now."

In the pasture behind the house, cows huddled around the massive bale of hay Mick had put out earlier. And as she moved onto the back porch, the sun peeked through the clouds, turning the rest of the field into a glittering mass of white.

She couldn't help taking a few more pictures. "Christa?"

Turning, she saw Mick pointing to the door. "Sorry." She quickly tucked the phone away, retrieved her keys and unlocked the door.

Dixie bounded into the house as though she was happy to be there, with Sadie right behind, followed by Christa and Mick.

It was only a few degrees warmer inside the house than it had been outside. However, the furnace was blowing, so her power had indeed been restored.

"I guess it'll take a while for things to warm up." While Mick closed the door, she moved past the kitchen table to check the thermostat in the living room. Thirty-nine degrees? At this rate, the furnace would be running nonstop for hours. "I should be fine, though." Shoving her gloved hands into the pockets of her coat, she returned to the kitchen to see Mick at the sink.

He turned on the water, but nothing happened. "I was afraid of that."

"What's wrong?" She stood beside him. "Is the pump still off?"

Lines creased his brow. "Pump's on. But your pipes are frozen." He let go a sigh. "I can't believe I didn't have you turn on all the faucets to drain the lines." Shaking his head, he pressed down on the lever that would normally turn off the water. "My brain must have frozen right along with my body."

"Why are you being so hard on yourself? So they're frozen. Won't they thaw out as the house warms up?"

"Yes, and that's when the trouble begins."

"Trouble?"

Wearing an exasperated look, he scowled down at her. "For someone who owns a hardware store, you don't know much about home repair."

Crossing her arms over her chest, she said, "Well, it would be nice if someone would just tell me what they're thinking instead of playing games."

"When water freezes it expands. There's likely frozen water in your pipes. That means those pipes have probably burst. Once the ice thaws—"

"Water will go everywhere." A sick feeling knotted her gut, while Mick's nod sent her heart plummeting. "If that's the case, then there's no way I can leave. I need to call a plumber." She reached for her phone.

"No plumber in his right mind is going to

get out on these roads." Why did he have to be so sensible?

"Okay, can we just turn the water off then?"

His expression softened, though she could tell he was thinking. "I s'pose. You'd still have some water leaking out as it thawed, but only what's in there now."

"Which means I might be able to avoid an all-out catastrophe."

"I reckon that might work. I've got a stash of pipe and fittings down at my place. Enough to do some crude repairs that'll tide you over until the plumber can get out here. Because I'm sure you won't be the only one with busted pipes."

"How do we figure out where the leaks are?"

"Tag-team it. Once things thaw, one of us turns on the water while the other watches for leaks. Then, once we spot one, we locate the break and cut the water back off. It'll still be a guessing game. And I'll have to put some holes in your walls. Maybe the ceiling."

"What?" Panic flitted through her veins.

"Don't shoot the messenger. A plumber would have to do the same thing."

She rubbed her forehead. "Please tell me insurance will cover this."

"It will."

At the moment, that was little comfort, but at least it was something.

"Look—" he placed his gloved hands on her shoulders, sending a jolt of electricity ricocheting through her "—let's just turn the pump off and go back down to my place where it's warm. Temps are supposed to inch above freezing overnight, so maybe things will have started to melt by morning, then we can address the breaks."

Staring into his green eyes, she felt plenty warm right here. "You're sure? I mean, I just finished renovating. I'd hate for things to get damaged. And these floors." She forced herself to step away and focus on the original wooden planks. "I couldn't bear it if they warped."

"Yeah, that's hundred-and-fifty-year-old longleaf pine." Lifting his gaze, he seemed to take in the entire space. "It's been a long time since I've been in here. With the lights on, that is." He sent her a quick smile.

Moving toward the living room, he continued to study things. "This is nice. Real nice. Hardly looks like the same place."

She recalled the mauve floral-striped wallpaper and dusty blue carpet that had been here the first time she saw the house, trying to ignore the spark of feelings his praise stirred inside her. Something warm and giddy. Something she hadn't felt in a long time. And promised herself she'd never feel again.

Yet Mick was suggesting she go back to the camp house with him and Sadie. How was she supposed to do that?

Get a grip, Christa.

She drew in a deep breath. *Lord, what is wrong with me?* It must be the stress of these last couple of days.

"Miss Christa?"

She looked down to see Sadie peering up at her, holding a box. "What is it, sweetheart?"

"I finded this puzzle on the shelf over there." She pointed toward the living room.

Christa took hold of the box bearing a picture of several golden retriever puppies and laughed. "My friend Paisley gave that to me for Christmas. I had just gotten Dixie, so she said she *had* to get it for me. I haven't had time to put it together yet, though."

"We could take it back to Uncle Mickey's and do it together." Her smile widened. "I love puzzles."

"I do, too," said Christa. "And you know what else Paisley gave me?"

"What?" Sadie's green eyes sparkled.

Christa crossed to the television. "This." She held up a DVD case.

"Frozen!" The child's entire face beamed. "I *love* that movie."

"Me, too." She glanced toward Mick, who

was still standing in the opening between the kitchen and living room, looking rather confused. "Maybe we could watch it while we're working on the puzzle."

"Yes, please." Sadie jumped up and down.

With her wayward feelings now in check, Christa approached the suddenly chagrined cowboy. "I'm ready when you are."

"You're trying to torture me, aren't you?"

"Have you ever even seen *Frozen*?"

"No, and I was hoping I'd never have to."

"Well, Uncle Mickey, looks like neither of us are getting our way today. I'm coming back to your place and you're going to watch *Frozen*."

"That should do it." Mick gathered his tools late the next morning, grateful that the only leaks they'd discovered at Christa's were in the kitchen, behind the washer and in the downstairs bathroom. That was, unless there was a holdout somewhere. He glanced Christa's way. "Why don't you go ahead and turn the water back on before I move this washer and dryer back into place."

"I'm on it."

As Christa disappeared out the door, Sadie's voice echoed from the living room. She'd asked to watch that *Frozen* movie again while he and

Christa worked and was singing along at the top of her lungs.

Chuckling to himself, he turned his attention to the window and watched Christa pick her way through the slush and mud in her backyard. Temperatures had climbed into the upper thirties overnight then shot into the forties once the sun came up, turning their winter wonderland into a sloppy mess. By midweek, the storm would be nothing but a memory. He hoped it'd be a happy one for Sadie, just as it was for him.

To his surprise, he'd rather enjoyed these last couple of days. For a guy who'd been single forever, he would've thought that having someone—a woman, no less—invade his space would have him climbing the walls. Now he almost hated to see Christa go. Though he was certain that was only because of Sadie. Christa never seemed to be at a loss for ideas to keep his niece busy. If it had been just him, the poor kid probably would have been bored the entire time.

He let go a sigh as Christa started back toward the house. Now that she was home, he and Sadie would have to restart their journey to finding a new norm. For him, that meant a life that encompassed both parenthood and ranching. Not to mention a *lot* of prayer. Because while he knew ranching, being responsible for another human being, a little girl at that, was uncharted territory for him. And knowing that the Sandersons were just waiting for him to fail so they could swoop in and take Sadie only increased the pressure.

Christa burst through the door. "How does it look?"

He eyed the hole he'd had to cut in the wall to access the pipes. "I think we're good to go."

"You're sure? I mean, what if another leak crops up?"

"Then just holler and I'll come back and fix it."

"But I was planning to head to the hardware store."

"Well, I reckon you could turn the water off until you get home."

She crossed her arms over her chest and rubbed them. "I guess that would work."

He'd never seen her look so nervous. Then again, she'd done lot of work on this house, making it look like a real farmhouse should. Not the 1980s country cottage look his mom had tried to achieve or the pristine white so-called farmhouse even city dwellers yearned for these days.

No, Christa had done right by this house. Yet other than the kitchen, where she'd replaced the worn plywood cabinets with a rustic quarter sawn oak version, she hadn't added much at all. Instead, she'd removed things, such as the carpet and dark wood paneling that had lined the walls of the living and dining rooms and the kitchen. Then she'd simply enhanced the old shiplap walls with a pale gray-green paint and returned the original wooden floors to their former glory.

A far cry from what he'd expected when she bought the place. He figured she'd make it all sleek and modern. But this? This was the way the house was meant to be.

A cozy place he wouldn't mind lingering in for a while. If he didn't have work to do.

But he did. It was time for things to get back to normal. Something that hadn't existed since the day he learned of Jen's death. In the blink of an eye, everything had changed. Life was no longer just about him. He had Sadie to consider. Yet ranching was his livelihood. He still had no idea how to mesh the two.

"Just let me get these appliances pushed back into place and Sadie and I will get out of your hair." He shimmied the dryer into position first, then the washer. "Come on, Sadie, it's time to go."

She bounded into the kitchen, all smiles. "Go where?"

"We need to check on the cattle and put out some more hay."

Her bottom lip pooched out then, her arms crossing defiantly over her chest. "I don't want to do that. I want to stay with Miss Christa."

Christa smoothed a hand over Sadie's hair. "Sorry, sweetie, I have to go to work, too. I have a store to run."

Tears welled in Sadie's eyes. Her lip trembled. "What about Dixie?"

"She's used to staying by herself," said Christa.

The dam broke loose then, and Sadie began to wail. "But I don't want to leave."

Mick's entire being cringed. He'd never been able to stand up to tears, even when Jen was little and would cry because she *wanted* to go with him and his dad, and Mom wouldn't let her. He knew he couldn't let Sadie get her own way, but he had no clue what to do.

He knelt in front of his niece. "Aw, come on, Sadie. Don't do this to me. Tell you what, once we're finished, I'll let you watch whatever you want."

She shook her head, grunting her displeasure.

Mick pushed to his feet. *Lord, I could use a little help here.* How on earth was he ever going to pull off ranching *and* raising Sadie? Sure, things were fine when she was in school, but what about weekends and breaks? And he didn't even want to think about summer.

"I sure wish I didn't have to go to work." Christa raised her voice enough to be heard over the tumult. "Mick, you've got some really cute baby calves out there." She sent him a look that told him to play along.

"Uh, yeah. Another one was born during the storm, too."

"Aw, poor baby. I hope it's all right."

"I do, too." He decided to play it up then. "But I don't know. It was mighty cold, and the weather's kept me from being able to check on it as often as I should."

"It's probably hungry." Christa cast a sideways glance as Sadie's cries grew quiet.

"Maybe starvin'," Mick added for good measure.

"And who knows—" Christa grabbed her jacket "—there could be another baby out there by now."

"Could be."

Sadie sniffed. Swiped the backs of her hands across her eyes. "I want to see the baby cow."

"You'll have to go with Uncle Mickey, then."

Why did he get the feeling Christa got a kick out of calling him Uncle Mickey? Still, she'd come to his rescue once again. And for that, he was grateful.

He looked down at his niece. "Maybe when

we're finished we can run into town and buy some more ice cream."

Sadie's green eyes widened. "Chocolate?"

"And sprinkles, too."

She smiled wide then. "I like sprinkles."

"I know you do." He helped her into her coat. "All right, Christa, looks like we're out of here." Glancing over his shoulder, he mouthed the words *Thank you*.

"You two have fun."

Fun would be awesome, but at this point, he was just happy the tears were gone.

Chapter Six

Christa crossed the parking lot of Bliss Community Church after service Sunday morning, taking pleasure in the birdsong that rang through the large oak trees surrounding the steepled brick building. A brilliant blue sky and temps in the fifties had erased virtually all signs of the ice storm. Yes, things were almost back to normal. And though the plumber would still need to make the permanent repairs to her pipes, and the holes she and Mick had to make in the walls to get to the pipes would have to be fixed, for the most part, her life could go on just the way it had before the storm.

Or so she thought. But something had changed. Much the way that year she'd spent caring for her father had changed her. As his cancer progressed, he kept reminding her not to overlook the simple things in life and to put others before herself. That's what had prompted her to step away from the corporate world for good and start a new life in Bliss.

This time, though, it had to do with a precious little brown-haired girl who had woven her way into Christa's heart, exposing a long-buried yearning for love, acceptance, family.

She drew in a breath of fresh air. Sure she had Dixie and Paisley, Rae and Laurel, but suddenly she found herself longing for more.

"Miss Christa, look at my picture."

She was halfway to her SUV when she heard Sadie calling. Dismissing her fanciful thoughts, she turned to see the beautiful child hurrying toward her, arms held wide, a piece of purple paper waving back and forth in one hand.

"Good morning." She stooped and caught the girl in a brief hug, savoring her sweetness. When she finally released her, she said, "Now what's this about a picture?"

Sadie proudly showed it to her. "See—" she pointed "—it's you, me, Dixie and Uncle Mickey in the ice storm."

Christa took in the abundance of white that looked more like a blizzard. Then again, from Sadie's perspective, it had probably looked like a blizzard. "You've even got Dixie smiling."

"Yeah, she smiles a lot." A winded Sadie giggled. "That's why I love her so much."

Christa stood as Mick approached, curious as to why he was frowning.

"Young lady." Lines creased his brow as he peered down at Sadie, looking none too happy. "What's the big idea running away from me? You know you're not supposed to be in the parking lot alone."

"But I wasn't alone." Sadie appeared oblivious to his concern. "Miss Christa was here."

Christa had been so focused on Sadie, she hadn't even noticed that Mick wasn't around. But watching cars move past them now sent a chill down her spine. "I was in the parking lot, yes—" she looked down at Sadie "—but I didn't know you were until you called my name." Christa did her best to keep her expression stern. "You should have waited for your uncle."

"But he was busy talking and I sawed you leave." The child's bottom lip protruded. "I wanted to show you the picture I drawed."

Christa's heartstrings tangled into the biggest knot ever. How could she get upset with that?

Mick crouched beside Sadie. "Princess, you could have been hit by a car. I'm sorry I got distracted, but next time, *please* tell me what you need. Don't just go taking off by yourself. Okay?"

Sadie blinked away tears. "Okay."

After hugging her, Mick stood and smiled at Christa, threatening to take her breath away. The cowboy sure cleaned up well. Dark washed Wranglers with a crisp crease were paired with a maroon-and-white-plaid shirt and separated by a rodeo-style silver belt buckle. Hands resting on Sadie's shoulders, he said, "How were things at the store?"

"Fine." She blew out a breath. "And the cattle?" She'd prayed all the way into town yesterday that Sadie would not only cooperate but enjoy checking cattle with Mick.

"I got to see *two* babies." Sadie held up two fingers for emphasis.

"And were they cute?"

"*So* cute. I nameded the white one Winter and the brown one Freckles because he had white spots on his face." She giggled.

"That sounds perfectly logical to me." And made her wish she could have gone with them. Things had felt pretty lonely when she arrived home last night. Even Dixie had seemed rather lost.

Being at the store, however, had reminded her about Sadie's room, something that seemed to have fallen by the wayside with the storm. So she distracted herself by playing with a design on her computer.

"Before I forget." She reached into her purse,

pulled out a folded piece of paper with the computer rendering of Sadie's new room and handed it to Mick. Since they hadn't said anything to Sadie about it, she simply said, "You can look it over and let me know what you think."

He didn't wait, though. He excitedly opened it right there, his eyes growing wide. "You can do this?" His look of utter amazement had her feeling a little unsteady.

"Sure. It's all cosmetic."

His smile faltered. "But what if…?"

She knew what he was getting at even if he couldn't finish the sentence. He was worried about the lawsuit and the possibility of losing Sadie to the Sandersons.

Lifting a shoulder, she said, "It's up to you. But I say think positive."

The corners of his mouth tipped upward in appreciation. "Do you mind if I—?" He nodded in Sadie's direction.

"Of course not."

He knelt again. "How would you like it if your new bedroom looked like this?" He turned it so she could see.

A smile illuminated Sadie's sweet face. "I would love it *so* much!"

Peering up at Christa, he stood. "I think we have our answer. When can you start?"

While she'd contemplated doing laundry this

afternoon, it didn't hold that much appeal. Besides, Dixie would be thrilled to spend some more time with Sadie.

"I don't have anything planned this afternoon. I could run over to the store now and mix the paint then come by after lunch."

"Little lady, if you're gonna do all this, the least I can do is buy you lunch."

She cleared her throat, her gaze narrowing. "Mick, if you call me little lady one more time, I might have to hurt you."

His mischievous grin made those green eyes sparkle. "Is that a threat?"

"I don't make threats, Mick. Only promises."

"Well, I promised Sadie that we'd grab burgers at Bubba's after church. Care to join us?"

"Please, please, please." Sadie pressed her little hands together.

"But I have to get the paint."

"That's all right." Taking hold of Sadie's hand, he continued. "You get the paint while we grab the burgers and we'll meet back at your place."

Telling herself that the excitement she felt bubbling inside her was simply because she could relate to Sadie, empathize with what she was going through in a way few people could, she said, "Sounds like a plan." Her gaze moved from Sadie to Mick. "I'll see you in a bit." Turning, she started for her vehicle.

"What should I get you?" Mick hollered after her.

She faced him again. "Bacon cheeseburger. No veggies. Mustard only." She started to retreat, then paused. "And a large fry, please."

"You got it, little lady." He sent her a wink that enticed as much as it irritated her. Making her wonder what she'd gotten herself into.

Mick's mind was a jumbled mess when he dropped Sadie off at school Monday morning and headed toward Rae's Fresh Start Café for a stiff cup of joe. As if the impending meeting with his attorney wasn't enough to make him nuts, images of Christa in that pretty red dress yesterday continued to pepper his brain. She'd looked so…feminine. Not at all like the jeans-and-T-shirt-clad Christa he was used to seeing. And for some strange reason, that confounded him.

Turning into the heart of Bliss, he eyed the courthouse square, noting the downed limbs that dotted the grounds. Between the winds and the weight of the ice, the old magnolia and live oak trees were bound to suffer some sort of damage. Fortunately, it wasn't too extensive and things would likely be cleaned up before the day was out.

He nabbed a parking spot in front of the row of late-nineteenth-century brick buildings opposite the courthouse and eased his truck to a stop. Lord willing, this turmoil rolling around inside him would be gone after his meeting. Because this shouldn't be a problem, right? Kyle and Jen had made sure everything was taken care of. *I*'s were dotted and *t*'s were crossed. So why were the Sandersons even trying?

Because Kyle's parents were used to things going their way.

The morning sun shone down on the town as he exited his truck and headed straight for the orange brick building that was Rae's. Inside, the smell of coffee mingled with bacon and syrup, something that normally would have awakened his appetite. But right now, black coffee was about all he could handle.

He eyed the table at the back of the restaurant where ranchers gathered every morning. The conversation appeared quite lively today. And if Mick were to make a guess, every bit of it centered around the storm. Things of that proportion didn't happen around these parts but once every few decades. It was the kind of thing that generated not only memories, but tall tales.

And he was certain a few of those were being born right now.

"Hey, Mick." Rae, the shop's owner, greeted him from behind the wooden counter on the left side of the room, while square wooden tables were scattered about the rest of the space. "You here to join the fellows?" She started to reach for a white mug.

"No, make mine to go today."

The pretty brunette pivoted toward the paper cups. "What size would you like?" Rae didn't need to ask *what* he wanted because all he ever got was just plain old coffee.

"A medium oughta do me." His gaze absently drifted to the chalkboard that hung on the exposed brick wall behind the counter, bearing a list of today's pastry offerings. Maybe he'd have to stop by after his meeting. Because once his appetite returned, he was sure those blonde brownies would be calling his name.

Watching Rae pour, he said, "When did you get back?" She, along with a few others from the church, had been in Costa Rica on a mission trip for the last two weeks.

"Late last night." She added a lid to the cup of steaming brew.

"And—" he retrieved his wallet from his back pocket "—how was it?"

Her entire face seemed to light up as she set

the cup on the counter. "Amazing. If I in any way touched those people's hearts as much as they did mine, I'll consider it successful."

He handed her enough to cover the coffee and tip. "Too bad you missed all the fun around here, though."

"Ha!" She opened the cash register. "If you're referring to the storm, I'm glad I wasn't here. I can do without cold and ice, thank you very much."

"It was an adventure." He tucked his wallet away. The two days he, Christa and Sadie had spent hunkered down at his place had been memorable for many reasons. Not the least of which was having the opportunity to get to know his beautiful neighbor a little better.

He touched the brim of his cowboy hat and grabbed the cardboard-sleeved cup. "Reckon I'd better go say hello to the fellas."

Bum stood and held out his hand as Mick neared the group. "Whatcha know, Mick?"

He shook his friend's hand. "Not much."

"Things gittin' back to normal?"

Mick rubbed the back of his neck. "Bum, I'm not even sure I know what normal is anymore."

The older man chuckled. "You'll figure it out, son." The front door opened, widening Bum's smile. "Well, look who's here."

Turning, Mick saw Christa heading toward

the counter, wearing jeans and a Bliss Hardware sweatshirt. Still, all he saw was that red dress from the other day.

He gave himself a stern shake as she started his way. "You'll have to excuse me, Bum."

Meeting him halfway, Christa looked concerned. "I thought you'd be at Cole's office."

"Not until nine. Figured I'd grab some caffeine." He gestured to the cup.

She peered up at him. "Are you nervous?"

Sucking in a breath, he thought for a moment. "The optimistic side of me isn't. Kyle and Jen stated in their will that they wanted me to raise Sadie. That should stand in a court of law. But the pessimist in me is scared to death. I've seen the news. I know things don't always turn out the way we think they should. Common sense is thrown aside, and decisions are made that defy logic."

"I'm sorry you're having to do this." Sincerity filled her hazel eyes. "I'll be praying."

"I appreciate that." More than she would ever know.

"Here you go, Christa," Rae called from behind the counter.

"Sorry, I've got to run. I'm just picking up an order I called in."

"That's all right. I should probably get on myself." He started toward the door as she picked up the drink carrier and fell in beside him.

"Keep me posted, okay?"

Opening the door for her, he said, "I will." He watched her head in the opposite direction, until she rounded the corner. Then he returned to his truck to retrieve the file folder of legal documents before moseying a few doors down to Cole Heinsohn's office. Though Cole had been four years ahead of Mick in school, they'd both grown up in Bliss and had become friends over the years. Cole was a no-nonsense kind of guy, so Mick knew he could count on Cole to be honest with him.

He pushed open the dark green door and stepped inside the office.

"Hello, Mick." Brenda Myers looked up from the large wooden desk to his left.

"You doin' all right, Brenda?" He pushed the door closed behind him, eyeing the seating area opposite her desk.

"I sure am. Now that that ice is out of here."

Mick chuckled, wishing he could say the same. Instead, his life seemed to be in chaos.

"Hey there, Mick." Holding a tall, insulated travel cup in one hand, the dark-haired attorney strode across the dark green carpet, wearing a suit that made him look more like he belonged in Austin or Houston than Bliss. But then, lawyers did tend to dress a little nicer than ranchers. "Come on into my office."

Mick followed. "How's your father?"

Dementia had forced Mr. Heinsohn into a local nursing facility after Cole's mom passed away three years ago.

"About the same." Cole closed the door. "Doesn't know me or remember what happened yesterday." He motioned toward one of two chairs in front of his desk. "Have a seat."

Unlike his suit, Cole's office was understated and strictly business. College diplomas and other legal certificates were the only things on the plain beige walls. The dark wood desk held a computer and three neat stacks of folders, while the bookshelf in the corner was laden with law books.

Continuing around to the back side of the desk, Cole said, "I'm sorry to hear about Jen. I'm sure that came as quite a shock."

"You're not kidding." Mick set his hat on the empty chair beside him and ran a hand through his hair. "I don't think I've really even had time to process everything. What with bringing Sadie back here and then the storm and this stupid lawsuit." He gestured to the folder.

"Has the probate process been initiated yet?"

Mick shook his head as Cole eased into his leather chair. "I reckon you can add that to my bill." He shoved the folder across the desk. "Both Jen's and Kyle's wills, as well as the summons I received, are in there."

"All right." Cole opened the file. "Let me have a look."

Mick waited, rather impatiently, his right leg bobbing up and down. His palms began to sweat. He swiped them across his jeans, hating that he was so nervous. He didn't get nervous. He could stare down a bull without breaking a sweat. Yet these last few weeks he'd been turned inside out. And just when he thought things couldn't get worse, that he was finally adjusting, the bottom had dropped out.

"Your brother-in-law was quite thorough." Cole continued to stare at the papers.

"He was a Sanderson. Even if he didn't act like one, I'm sure it was ingrained in him to protect his assets." Who would have thought it was his parents he'd need the most protection from?

"Under normal circumstances, these wills would be considered straightforward." Cole looked him in the eye. "But I'm not going to kid you, Mick. The biggest problem here is *who* we're up against. I'm sure you know that nothing is ever easy with Chuck and Belita Sanderson."

"That's why Kyle was so adamant about having everything in order. Just in case."

"I have no doubt the Sandersons conferred with their lawyers before filing this suit. They wouldn't do it unless they thought they stood a chance of winning. That means we've got an uphill battle."

"Why? I mean, Kyle and Jen had all of this done a long time ago."

"And to us that seems reasonable. However, the grandparents are a two-parent household, are well-known throughout the state and have a lot of money. Meaning they can afford to drag this out until you throw up your hands in defeat."

A fire started in Mick's belly. He shot to his feet and leaned across the desk. "I would never do that, Cole. I made a promise to my sister. One I fully intend to keep."

Remaining calm, Cole looked up at him. "Even if you run out of money?"

Mick sank back into his seat. While he lived a comfortable life, he wasn't wealthy by any means. What if he ran out of resources? How far was he willing to go?

Seemed all he could do was pray it wouldn't come to that. Because if he lost Sadie, he wasn't sure what he'd do.

Chapter Seven

Christa clicked the Submit button on the computer screen in her office later that morning, successfully transmitting the order for a specialty door one of her customers wanted. Too bad she hadn't been able to help them with the flooring they also wanted.

What could possibly be taking that leasing agent so long? Five days and still no response.

Huffing out a breath, she rolled her chair across the colorful area rug and away from her white, sawhorse-style desk. At this rate, she'd never pull off an expansion before Cranes moved into the area.

Okay, so the building supply chain had yet to announce plans for a store near Bliss, but everyone knew it was coming. In the meantime, residents were forced to shop at the big home improvement centers in the city, when what they really wanted was to do business with merchants they knew and trusted.

She grabbed a piece of chocolate from the emergency stash she kept in a galvanized bucket atop the row of white two-drawer file cabinets. Savoring the peanut butter and chocolate confection, she stared out the small window, toward the store's front door, wondering how Mick's meeting had gone. It had been almost two hours since she ran into him at Rae's. Perhaps he and Cole were still talking. Or maybe Mick just figured he'd talk to Christa later, unaware of the fact that she was just as nervous as he was about this lawsuit. If it had been anyone else but the Sandersons doing the filing, she might not be so concerned. But the Sandersons had a pack of attorneys at their beck and call, no doubt ready to pounce on unsuspecting souls in order to make sure their clients came out on top. And so help her, if they tried to pull something underhanded with Mick—

The man in question walked into the store just then. Stepping out of her office, she waved to catch his attention and motioned him her way. He looked weary as he approached. As though the stress of the last few weeks had finally caught up to him.

He stepped inside her office and she promptly closed the door to keep their conversation private.

"How'd it go?" Crossing her arms, she leaned her backside against her desk as he dropped into one of the metal side chairs.

He shook his head, removed his hat and jammed a hand through his hair. "I think I'm in over my head, Christa."

She ached for this poor man who was trying so hard to do the right thing. Pouring himself into caring for his niece. "Why? Did something else happen?"

"No. It's just—hearing Cole lay out his concerns only amplified my own."

"Such as?"

"He's worried that the Sandersons will drag things out."

"That doesn't sound so bad. At least it'll keep Sadie with you."

"I think he was referring to the cost of a lengthy trial. Wearing me down, as Cole put it, until I run out of money."

She looked at him matter-of-factly. "That will never happen. Not as long as I'm around. And I guarantee the people of Bliss would rally around you, too. They'd be having bake sales, fried fish and barbecue suppers until they were blue in the face just to help raise money."

"He also said that a two-parent household can carry a lot of weight."

She puffed out an incredulous laugh. "Yeah,

if they're actually willing to raise the child and not pawn her off on nannies and boarding schools." Pushing away from the desk, she began to pace. "This whole thing irritates me to no end. As if a single man can't raise a child. Boy, I'd like to tell them a thing or two. After all, I was raised by a single man and I turned out just fine."

"There's no telling what the Sandersons will use as ammunition." Hands clasped, he rested his forearms on his denim-clad thighs. "Not just that I'm single, but the fact that I'm a rancher." He tilted his head to look at her. "As you've already figured out, I don't get days off."

"Could you hire somebody to help you? I know Bum was checking on things while you were gone to get Sadie."

"He was just doing me a favor. And about the only time we bring in help is when we work cattle, and that's usually a trade-off. They help me, then I turn around and help them." He fell quiet for a moment. "I have no doubt, though, that the Sandersons will likely harp on the fact that I have no help with Sadie. As in, I don't have a wife to care for her."

Every time he said that, Christa's blood boiled a little hotter. This time it had ignited an idea. "Fine, if that's the way they're going to be, then we'll just call their bluff."

Mick straightened, looking confused. "How?"

She sucked in a breath, finding it difficult to believe she was about to say this, but desperate times called for desperate measures. "Let's get married. You and me."

Mick's expression went from dumbfounded to completely horrified in a matter of seconds. "Woman, have you lost your mind?"

Ignoring the direct hit to her ego, she said, "Perhaps. But if that's what it takes to protect Sadie, then so be it."

Standing, he crossed to where she stood. "Christa, I appreciate what you're doing here, but you can't marry someone you don't love."

"Oh, as if there aren't plenty of married people who don't love each other. And I wasn't talking about moving in together or anything like that."

He set his hands on her shoulders. "No, you were thinking of a little girl who's been tossed around by enough of life's storms. And I admire you for that. But I would never dream of tying you down in some marriage of convenience. You're a beautiful, spirited woman who deserves to love and be loved."

Christa knew Mick was just being nice, that her suggestion they get married was totally ludicrous, yet staring up into his green eyes, she found herself wondering what it might be like to be loved and wanted by a good, hardworking man like him. To have someone you could lean on, count on to walk with you through life's troubles.

Shaking off the notion, she turned away, hoping Mick couldn't see the sudden heat in her cheeks. He probably thought that, given her age, she was desperate to get married and that was why she'd thrown out something so crazy.

"Sorry, I got a little caught up in my emotions. I guess, because of my own past, their supposition that you're not fit to raise Sadie feels rather personal."

"I understand. You don't want to see Sadie hurt."

"Or you." She had to force herself to look at him again, balling her fists so she wouldn't be tempted to rest her palms against his broad chest. "I'm willing to help you any way I can. If you need someone to watch Sadie, please don't hesitate to ask."

"You're sure?"

"Of course I'm sure."

"All right. I was just checking."

"Oh, and I'm still planning to come by to do that second coat of paint in her bedroom tonight. And I ordered the comforter set. It should be here tomorrow. Then I'll just need to gather a few more things to pull the room together before the big reveal."

Finally, he smiled. "Sadie's going to be excited."

Christa was, too. Except once Sadie's room was finished, she'd have no reason to see Mick or Sadie, unless Mick needed someone to watch her. And knowing that they would no longer be an everyday part of her life had her feeling rather sad.

"Look! It's Dixie and Miss Christa." Sadie's voice drifted from the back seat of Mick's truck as he approached the driveway on the way home from school Wednesday.

They hadn't seen Christa since Monday night when she'd finished painting Sadie's room. The change in color alone had completely transformed the space. But he and Sadie were eager to see the finished product in a few days.

Yeah, he was starting to realize just how special Christa was. If he thought for one moment he could win her heart, he just might have taken her up on her offer to get married. After all, she'd been so wonderful with Sadie. The two of them had really connected.

Yet Mick and Christa were as different as night and day. She was well-educated and sophisticated, while he was just a humble cowboy.

He'd learned the hard way that while women were enamored with the persona, they often found the man lacking. Christa would never be interested in someone like him.

So why was he still thinking about that whole exchange two days later?

"Dixie!" Sadie bounced in the back seat. "I wanna say hi."

"All right, princess." Turning into the drive, he eased to a stop and rolled his window down to the sounds of chattering birds. "You're home kinda early." Usually she didn't make it back from the store until after five thirty.

"Plumber's coming out." She neared the truck, a gentle breeze carrying her sweet scent into the cab.

"It took him this long?"

She lifted a petite shoulder. "We patched the pipes, so I guess he figured that bought him some time. Besides, it's not like I was the only person in the area with broken pipes."

"True." He rested his elbow on the door. "Who's coming out? Joe Lopez?"

"No, he hurt his back. Apparently he slipped on the ice, so I had to settle for Ronnie Cranston."

Mick's lip instinctively curled into a snarl while his heart pounded wildly with protectiveness. "*Cranston*? That creep's been hitting on you since you got to town. Why on earth would you want *him* in your house?"

Her hands went to her hips, her hazel eyes narrowing. "Ashford, are you under the mistaken impression that I'm unable to take care of myself?"

"No, I just don't trust *that* man in *your* house. What if he plants some of those hidden cameras somewhere?"

She puffed out a laugh. "I had no idea you had such an active imagination."

"When it comes to Cranston, there's not much I wouldn't put past him. Do you know how many times they caught him sneaking into the girls' locker room when we were in high school?"

She shifted uncomfortably. "How many?"

"Well, I don't remember exactly. But it was more than a couple."

"Come on, Mick. That was almost thirty years ago." Chewing her bottom lip, she crossed her arms over her chest. "Though it is kind of creepy. But he's already on his way out here, so it's not like I can cancel now."

"Can I go see Dixie?" Sadie had unbuckled her seat belt and was draped over his seat.

"Oh, sorry, princess." He pressed the button to unlock the doors.

She hopped out and hugged Christa around the waist.

"How was school?" Christa smoothed a hand over Sadie's back.

Squinting against the sun, she peered up at the woman. "We got to paint today."

The endearing way Christa looked at his niece as she cupped her cheek almost made Mick forget about the fact that Creepy Cranston was on his way out here.

"You know—" he rubbed the stubble on his chin "—this might be a real good time for Sadie and me to pay you a visit."

As Sadie knelt to hug Dixie, Christa turned her attention back to Mick. "Why?"

"Just seems like the neighborly thing to do. Besides—" he glanced toward his niece "—Sadie wants to spend some time with Dixie."

Cocking her head, Christa sent him a knowing look. "And it has nothing to do with the fact that Ronnie is on his way out here?"

"Are you kidding? It has everything to do with that. And if that creep tries to linger a little longer than he should, well, then we will, too, 'cause we're going out for dinner tonight."

"Don't you think you're overreacting?"

"No, ma'am. I will do whatever is necessary to keep you from being alone with Cranston."

He parked his truck in her drive, before following Christa and Sadie into the house.

"Do you have any cookies?" Sadie rubbed her belly. "I am *so* hungry."

Mick cringed. He'd forgotten Sadie usually had a snack when she got home.

"Sadie, we don't need to impose on Miss Christa. I'll run down to the camp house and grab you a juice box and granola bar." He turned for the door.

"You don't have to do that, Mick." Christa's words stopped him. "I've got some peanut butter cookies in the fridge I've been dying to make." She smiled at Sadie. "This'll be just the excuse I need." She opened the refrigerator door. "Because then I won't eat them all myself." She reached into the fridge before handing something to Sadie. "Here's a string cheese to tide you over—"

A knock sounded at the door.

Mick pulled out a chair at the table and made himself at home. "Looks like your plumber's here."

Christa shut the refrigerator door and started across the kitchen into the mudroom while Sadie crawled into the chair beside Mick and peeled the plastic wrapper off her cheese.

A moment later, the door opened.

"Hello, beautiful." Apparently Cranston wasn't

wasting any time. Had the guy not seen Mick's truck out there?

"Hey, Ronnie," said Christa. "I'm glad you're here."

"I know you are, darlin'." Creepy Cranston drew out each word, and it took every ounce of determination Mick had to stay seated.

Keep your cool. Just look like you belong here. Something that shouldn't be a problem, given that he'd grown up in this house. Still, visions of Cranston ogling Christa had Mick ready to pounce. It was almost as if he was—

No, that couldn't be it. Mick and Christa weren't a couple or anything. They weren't even dating, so why would Mick be jealous? No, he'd be gunning to protect any woman from Ronnie Cranston.

Except this wasn't *any* woman. It was Christa.

Finally she moved into the kitchen with Ronnie right on her heels.

Mick leaned back in his chair, clasping his hands behind his head. "Hello, Ronnie."

Cranston's dark gaze jerked to Mick's, as though he'd just been busted. "Ashford, what are you doing here?" He looked from Mick to Christa, no doubt wondering if they were a couple.

"Keepin' an eye on you. Makin' sure you behave like a gentleman."

"What are you talkin' about? I'm always a gentleman."

Mick fought the urge to laugh. "In that case, I'd best let you get to your work."

Pulling off a strip of cheese, Sadie twisted to look at Christa. "Are we still going to make the cookies?"

"We sure are. Just let me show Mr. Cranston which pipes need to be fixed."

"I can do that, Christa." Mick all but jumped at the opportunity. "You and Sadie go ahead and work on those cookies. I'll take care of ole Ronnie."

Once the water was turned off, Mick showed the fellow to the master bath.

"I didn't know you were sweet on Christa, Mick. Can't say as I blame you, though. She's a looker."

"Just stick to the pipes." He pointed toward the wall. "And I ain't sweet on her. We're just friends."

"Coulda fooled me. The only woman I recall you being that protective of was your sister. But if you're just friends, then I reckon you won't mind if I ask her out."

"'Course not. She'd just tell you no just like every other time."

His phone rang and Mick looked at the screen

to see Margaret Flannery's name. Margaret was an older widow he leased pastureland from.

He pointed toward the hole in the wall. "Just get to work." Turning, he touched the screen to accept the call as he moved into the blue-and-white bedroom and pressed the phone to his ear. "Hello."

"Mick, I know you're probably all kinds of busy, but I thought I should let you know that I just passed one of your cows out on the road. A pretty brown and white one that would make a gorgeous rug someday."

He pinched the bridge of his nose. Talk about bad timing. If a cow was out, he had no choice but to go and put her back in. Not to mention check the fence line to see how she got out in the first place, then make any necessary repairs. Because if the animal caused any sort of accident, either someone hitting it or swerving to miss it, Mick was the one who'd be held responsible.

"Whereabouts, Margaret?"

"Right there at the bend by Duck's Hollow."

"I'll head over there now. Thanks for letting me know."

He made his way back into the kitchen where Christa and Sadie were setting the pieces of dough onto a cookie sheet. "I have to leave."

Christa looked his way. "Problem?"

"I've got a cow out on the road."

"Well, you'd better go take care of her." She smiled and nodded toward Sadie. "We'll be fine here."

"Are you sure?" He gestured in the general direction of her bathroom, where Cranston had better be focusing on the pipes and nothing else.

"I'm a big girl, Mick. Besides, Sadie will be here."

He supposed a five-year-old would be a good buffer, if not an effective deterrent. "I'll be back just as quick as I can."

It didn't take him long to locate the Red Angus mix grazing in the ditch, along with the section of barbed wire that a tree limb had taken down, probably during the storm. He coaxed the cow back inside, then grabbed his pliers, wire stretcher and gloves from his truck and repaired the section. He'd have to come back with his chain saw later to remove the tree. But for now, he needed to get back to Christa and Sadie. He'd promised to take them to dinner, after all.

His hackles went up when he saw Cranston's truck still in Christa's drive almost an hour after Mick had left. And for the life of him, he couldn't figure out why he felt so strongly about protecting Christa. Like she said, she was a grown woman. One who was definitely no pushover. She'd gone toe-to-toe with Mick on more than one occasion and never failed to hold her own.

The only woman I recall you being that protective of was your sister.

As much as he hated to admit it, Cranston was right. And Mick wasn't quite sure what to make of that.

When he knocked on the door, it was Ronnie who opened it instead of Christa.

"I'm just finishing up." He motioned to the gaping hole behind the washer.

"Good." Mick moved past him and continued into the kitchen where the sweet smell of peanut butter still hung in the air. "Don't suppose you saved me a cookie, did you?"

"Uncle Mickey!" Sadie looked up from the table. "Miss Christa letted me paint my fingernails." She held up her hands to reveal pink-and-blue-tipped fingers.

His gaze drifted to Christa who was sitting beside her. "You're a brave woman."

"Smart, too." She pushed her chair back and stood. "It's water based, so it peels right off." She demonstrated with her own fingers then pointed toward the counter. "And yes, we saved you some cookies."

He crossed to the small island and grabbed a couple.

"All right, folks."

Cookie in hand, Mick turned to see Cranston standing in the doorway between the kitchen and mudroom.

"I'm going to turn the water back on. If there are no leaks, you should be good to go."

"Excellent." Christa looked at Mick. "Now I get to learn drywall repair."

By the time Ronnie pulled away, the sun was drifting low in the western sky and Mick's stomach was ready for something more than cookies.

He watched Christa as she cleared off the table. "So where would you like to go eat?"

"Honestly—" she wadded up the waxed paper she'd laid out to protect the wood finish while they did their nails "—I'm not really in the mood to go anywhere."

Disappointment settled in his gut, surprising him.

"However—" Christa tucked the paper in the trash before facing him again "—if you don't mind frozen pizza, we could eat here."

The offer lifted his spirits. He enjoyed Christa's company. Her outlook on life, her values were very similar to his, which had him thinking that maybe they weren't so different after all. And that made frozen pizza too good to resist.

Chapter Eight

~❧~

Christa pulled her SUV up to Mick's house Friday evening, eager to show Sadie her completed room. She'd taken a long lunch today so she could finish the project. With the painting out of the way, it hadn't taken long to style the wall shelves she'd had Mick put up, rearrange the furniture and add some fun wall art along with the new bedding. The space was now colorful, inviting and, most of all, designed specifically for Sadie.

The only downside was that it meant she no longer had a reason to come down to Mick's place and hang out with him and Sadie. It had felt rather strange being there earlier with both of them gone. Almost as if she was invading their turf by introducing items she was certain Mick never dreamed of having in his house.

He'd be okay, though, because she wasn't changing things for his benefit, but for Sadie's.

Christa enjoyed watching the two of them together. She never would have guessed that the tough cowboy she'd always encountered could be turned inside out by one little girl. But he was so sweet with Sadie. As if he was meant to be a father.

Christa released a sigh. What would she do now that Sadie's room was complete?

Start pestering her real estate agent, for one thing. She couldn't believe there was still no word on the Gebhardt building. Perhaps Christa should try to contact the leasing agent directly. Maybe that would get the ball rolling.

Determining that was a decision for another day, she got out of her vehicle then opened the back door. "There you go, Dixie."

The dog hopped out and started exploring, nose to the ground.

Christa waited, taking in the picturesque setting. With the large trees and the pond, she could see why Mick liked living here. She could just imagine sitting at the water's edge, watching Sadie splash around with Dixie.

Her heart skidded to a stop. Once Mick found his footing as a parent, he'd have no need for Christa anymore. That was, assuming the court case came out in his favor.

She sucked in a breath. *Father God, please let Sadie remain with Mick. He's trying so hard and he loves her so much.*

"Come on, Dix." Turning, she continued onto the porch and knocked on the door. A moment later, a haggard Mick swung it open.

"Boy, am I glad you're here."

She could hear Sadie crying. Make that screaming.

She stepped inside. "What's going on?" Her gaze shifted to the living room where Sadie lay on the floor throwing one doozy of a tantrum.

"I wish I knew. Ever since I picked her up from school, all she's done is argue. Whatever I ask her to do, she says no. I even told her she was going to get to see her new room tonight, but she had to wait until you got here. So she threw herself on the floor and has been kicking and screaming ever since."

"That doesn't sound like Sadie."

"I know." Mick dragged a hand through his light brown hair. "I'm 'bout at my wit's end. She won't talk to me. And whenever I try to talk to her, she screams louder."

Another screech rent the air.

Something was amiss. And Christa hadn't had enough experience with kids to know how to handle this. Still, she had to give it a try.

She moved tentatively toward the girl and

crouched to her level. "Sadie? Hey—" she brushed the child's shoulder-length hair out of her reddened face "—what's going on?"

Sadie jerked away and continued to scream and sob.

Standing, Christa glanced at Mick, who looked every bit as helpless as she felt. "Did something happen at school?"

"Not that I'm aware of."

Christa looked down at the child, hating to see her so upset. There had to be a reason for an outburst like this. And the only way they were going to find out was for Sadie to tell them. But how could they get her to do that?

A few tumultuous moments passed before Christa decided to join Sadie on the floor. And despite the protests, she pulled the thrashing child into her lap. "Come on, Sadie. Talk to me. What's the problem?" Despite the child's continued kicking, Christa drew her closer. "Don't you want to see your new room?"

"*No!* I don't want a new room!"

Willing herself to remain calm, Christa breathed deep and kept her voice even. "Okay, what do you want then?"

"I want my mommy and daddy!"

Christa's gaze collided with Mick's, her insides churning with grief—for Sadie and the little girl Christa had been. Tears sprang to her eyes as she recalled that night when her emotions had come to a head and she'd fallen apart on her father. The ache in her little heart had been more than she could take. She couldn't remember what had set her off, only that she'd lost it and there'd been nothing her father could do to console her. She'd been too young to understand what was going on; she only knew that she'd wanted her mother. And she was certain that's what Sadie was enduring right now.

In that moment, Christa understood just how helpless her father had felt. But that hadn't stopped him from trying to console her. And she would do the same for Sadie.

Ignoring the girl's continued flailing, Christa hugged her tight and smoothed a hand over her tangled hair. "I know you do, baby. I know you miss them." She whispered in Sadie's ear, "Your mommy and daddy loved you so much. I know you don't understand why they had to go away."

The kicking began to subside and the tension in Sadie's body started to ease.

"I know you miss them terribly," Christa continued, determined to ride out this storm with the precious child in her arms.

After a moment, Sadie turned into Christa's chest, her body shaking with each hiccup as Christa cradled her. Through tears, she peered up at her. "Why did they leave me?"

"They didn't want to, baby." If only there was an answer suitable for a five-year-old. "Just like my mommy didn't want to leave me. But sometimes things just happen." Tears spilled onto her cheeks.

Sadie reached up and caught one on her finger.

Christa sniffed and tried to keep herself from falling completely apart. "And your Uncle Mickey loves you so very much."

He joined them on the floor then, his own face wet with tears, and Christa could feel the heat radiating from him as he drew close.

His shoulder touched hers as his calloused hand tenderly stroked Sadie's hair. "I miss your mama and daddy, too, Sadie." His voice cracked. "Your mama was my best friend."

Sadie sat up in Christa's lap and twisted to look at her uncle. With a sniff, she said, "She was?"

"Would I lie to you?"

Sadie thought for a moment before shaking her head.

"And I promised your mama and daddy that I would take care of you. So I really need you to talk to me when something is bothering you. It's okay to cry and get upset, but it would sure help me if I knew why you were doing it. Even if I can't make it better."

Christa smoothed a hand over Sadie's back. "Do you think you can do that, Sadie? Tell your Uncle Mickey when you're feeling sad or mad?"

The child was still for a moment before she reached for Mick.

Christa's heart split wide open when he pulled his niece close, hugging her for all she was worth, while tears streamed down his face. Oh, how she prayed the Sandersons wouldn't tear them apart. She couldn't bear what it might do to these two precious souls.

The three of them sat there, silently working through their grief, until Dixie sidled over and sat down beside Mick, as though she was waiting for Sadie.

"Dixie." Sadie pulled away and smiled at the dog. Then she placed a tiny hand on each of her uncle's cheeks. "I love you, Uncle Mickey."

"I love you, too, princess." He kissed her cheek.

Sadie looped an arm around Dixie's neck and turned to Christa. "I'm ready to see my new room now."

Laughing through her tears, Christa said, "We can do that. But first, I think we need a round of tissues."

Mick wasn't about to break his arm trying to pat himself on the back, but peering at his watch as he stood on his front porch Sunday afternoon, he realized that he'd almost made it through his first somewhat normal weekend alone with Sadie. And as far as he was concerned, that was something to celebrate.

They'd spent Saturday morning putting out hay. At each of the five pastures, he'd eyeball the herd, make sure every cow and bull were accounted for, that none were having any issues, and then double-check the mamas with babies, as well as those that would be calving soon.

After church today, they'd grabbed lunch at Bubbas and ate in the truck as they made the rounds again. Sadie had been the first to spot a new calf, which she had to name, just like all the others. Unlike yesterday, though, she'd fallen asleep on the way back to the house. So he'd carried her to the couch, then settled into his recliner for a catnap of his own.

Now it was closing in on three o'clock. Meaning they still had plenty of time to do something fun. It would be a shame to waste such a beautiful, spring-like day.

"Sadie, how would you like to go horseback riding?"

Surprise lit her face as she hopped out of the porch's lone rocker. "I would love, love, love it!"

He'd picked up a helmet for her at the farm supply this week, anticipating such a ride. She'd only been talking about it since they returned from the funeral. And this was the perfect day to be out and about and to start building some memories. Just in case—

No, he was not going to let thoughts of the Sandersons ruin this day.

"You'll have to ride with me, though."

"Okay." She nearly bounced right out of her pink boots.

"All right, let's call Drifter in."

Sadie cupped her hands around her mouth and yelled for the horse, while Mick simply curled in his lips and let go a whistle.

A few minutes later, the sorrel mare wandered in from the pasture.

Sadie smiled up at him. "She heareded me."

"She sure did." No sense in bursting the kid's bubble by telling her Drifter knew his whistle. Because slowly but surely, Sadie was easing into country life. Mick had been pleased to see that Christa hadn't forgotten that when she decorated Sadie's room. The horseshoe lamp and cowhide-looking pillow were a nod to his way of life. He appreciated that.

Naturally, Sadie had fallen in love with the space. Mick knew she would. And anything that made Sadie happy made him happy.

Christa had a knack for making Sadie happy. Rubbing his chin, he pondered his beautiful neighbor. Now that Sadie's room was complete, she had no reason to visit them anymore. And though he'd never admit it to anyone but himself, he missed having her around. Because whenever she was there, things seemed different. Better. Even when things got bad, like they had Friday night.

In all the chaos of this past month, Mick had never truly grieved his sister and the man who'd been like a brother to him. But the other night, the wall he'd built around his heart had come crumbling down as he watched Sadie struggle with her new reality. And while it wasn't exactly manly to cry in front of a woman—a pretty one at that—it felt right for Christa to be there. She understood what he and Sadie were going through. And he couldn't help feeling as though God had placed her in their lives to help them work through this difficult time. Something Mick would be forever thankful for.

After saddling Drifter and briefly explaining the process to Sadie, he retrieved the helmet he'd stowed in the barn. "You'll need to wear this while we're riding."

"I like the pink." Taking the helmet from him, she studied it for a moment. "Oh, and it has a unicorn on it. I like that." She looked up at him. "How come I don't have a hat like you?"

"Because you're still growing, so we have to

protect that pretty little head of yours." Besides, if Jen were here, she'd give him a good tongue-lashing if he let Sadie ride without a helmet.

Thankfully, Sadie didn't argue, and in no time they were atop Drifter and headed up the drive with Sadie's little body tucked in front of his.

"We need to go to Miss Christa's so she can see me on a horse."

"Do we now?" He couldn't seem to stop the smile that tugged at his lips. "I reckon we can do that."

When they emerged from the woods, Christa's farmhouse was bathed in sunlight. The windows were open, and a gentle breeze billowed the sheer white curtains inside.

The horse whinnied as they neared the drive.

"Sounds like Drifter is as eager to see Miss Christa as you are." Not that Mick wasn't looking forward to it, too.

The woman in question appeared at the dining room window. "What are you doing?"

"I'm riding a horse." Pride filled Sadie's voice.

"You sure are. Give me a second. I want to take your picture."

Mick guided Drifter alongside the fence.

"Right there is good."

He looked up to see Christa tiptoeing across

the cattle guard, her faithful furry companion by her side. She wore a pair of denim overalls over a gray T-shirt, and her chin-length brown hair was slightly mussed, making him wonder what she'd been doing before they arrived.

"Hold on." He angled the horse just so. "How's that?"

"Perfect. Now smile." Using her phone, she took several pictures then stared at the screen. "These are great." She looked their way. "I'll have to frame a couple of them."

Frame? As in display, like in her house or office? And why did that make him sit a little taller in the saddle?

"I'll text them to you so you can have them, too." She slid her phone into her pocket.

"Miss Christa, can I play on your swing?" Sadie pointed to the simple board-and-rope swing that dangled from the sprawling live oak in the front yard.

"You sure can." She stepped closer, holding out her arms as Mick passed Sadie down. "I like your helmet." She stood Sadie on the ground as Mick dismounted.

"Uncle Mickey gotted it for me." She hugged Dixie then turned to leave.

Mick snagged her arm. "Hold up a second." He stooped so he was at her level. "Always walk in front of a horse—" he pointed "—not behind."

"How come?"

"So you don't get kicked."

Her eyes widened.

"No matter how nice a horse may be, if they see something behind them, they're apt to kick. It's how they protect themselves."

"Ooh…" She eyed Drifter. "But they don't kick in the front?"

"Nope."

She smiled then. "Okay." She skipped around the front end of the horse and continued across the cattle guard to the swing.

"That was good." Christa stepped closer. "Teaching her about horses, the helmet."

"I'm just glad I remembered. Sometimes I forget that she didn't grow up on a ranch like Jen and I did."

"You'll just have to act as though everything is new. That is, until the day she looks up at you and says, '*I know, Uncle Mickey.*'"

"Let's hope that day doesn't come anytime soon." He glanced at the cattle in the winter-brown pasture behind her house. "What have you been up to?"

"Drywall repair."

Lifting a brow, he met her gaze. "All by yourself?"

"All by myself."

"How's it going?"

"Surprisingly, not too bad. Though there's definitely a learning curve to applying that joint compound."

"No doubt." He took a step closer, staring at the top of her head. "However, that does explain something."

She looked up at him as he drew closer. "What?"

"Just hold still." The sweet aroma of her shampoo—apple, maybe—enveloped him as he cupped her chin with one hand while pinching the small white blob that had affixed itself to the top of her head with the other. Her hair was soft, and the fragrance radiating from her had him entertaining notions he had no business entertaining. Like the fact that she was close enough to kiss. And what would she do if he did?

Clearing his throat, he took a step back, revealing the joint compound. "Were you saving this for later?"

Her hands immediately went to her hair. "How did that get there?"

"I have no idea."

She smiled then and poked a thumb toward the house. "Would you like to see my patch job?"

"Sure."

They moved into the yard where Sadie was draped over the swing, her belly against the wood instead of her bottom.

"Miss Christa and I are gonna run inside for a minute. You want to come with us?"

"Me and Dixie want to stay here and swing." With the dog sitting beside her, Sadie pushed off again, lifting her feet into the air so as not to impede her movement.

"Okay. I'll be right back." He followed Christa into the mudroom and kitchen where she proudly showed off her handiwork. He met her gaze. "And you've never done this before?"

"No, sir."

"I guess you're one of those naturals then, because you can't even tell there was a hole there."

Her cheeks went pink. "Well, maybe not once it's painted."

"I'm proud of you."

"Thanks." Her gaze met his, and he quickly realized just how much he'd missed being with her.

"Say, would you—"

Worry creased her brow as she held up a hand. "Do you hear crying?" She turned for the door. "Sadie?"

Mick followed her outside and down the steps with Sadie's sobs meeting his ears.

In the front yard, Sadie sat on the ground

cradling her arm. Her face was red, and tears streaked down her cheeks.

"What happened, honey?" Christa dropped to her knees beside the child.

Mick did the same, his heart wrenching. Why had he left her?

"My arm!" Sadie wailed.

Finding his voice, he said, "Show me where it hurts."

She pointed to her forearm, her cries decreasing in volume as Christa soothed her.

He carefully ran a hand over the area, looking for any obvious protrusions or such. "Can you do this?" He held his hand out, palm down.

Sadie mimicked him.

"Now do this." He rotated it so his palm was facing up.

Sadie started to turn it, only to cry out in pain.

His gaze slammed into Christa's. "I need to get her to the hospital."

"I'll drive."

Mick scooped Sadie into his arms. "This is all my fault."

Christa stepped in front of him. "No, it's not. It was an accident."

"I never should have left her alone." And if the Sandersons got wind of this, he'd lose Sadie for sure.

Chapter Nine

It's only a minor sprain.

Using her utility knife, Christa sliced open a cardboard container of wood screws Tuesday afternoon, certain the doctor had no idea what a mountain of guilt that seemingly innocent statement had carried. And even though Sadie had confessed that she'd been standing on the swing, Mick was still beating himself up when Christa ran into him at Rae's earlier this morning.

She pulled out several small plastic tubs, hating that he was being so hard on himself. Especially when Sadie's fall had been just as much Christa's fault. Maybe even more, since she was the one who'd invited him inside. It never even crossed her mind that Sadie could get hurt on something as benign as a tree swing that was only two feet off the ground. How foolish could she be?

Yet instead of owning up to her guilt, she'd taken them a basket filled with trinkets, snacks and homemade treats after work last night. Having fretted over the child all day, she wanted to see for herself how Sadie was doing. Thankfully, the kid didn't appear too worse for the wear. She was pretty proud of her sling, but disappointed she hadn't gotten a pink cast that everyone could sign.

Christa had emptied the box and was stacking the last of the tubs atop the metal shelf when Patsy came around the corner of aisle six.

"I just heard something you're *not* gonna like."

No doubt some tidbit of gossip on one of Bliss's residents. Though how that would impact Christa, she wasn't sure.

She sliced the tape on the bottom of the box, flattened it and added it to the growing pile beside her before addressing her assistant manager. "And that would be?"

"Gordon Winslow was just here." Patsy planted her fists on her curvaceous hips.

"Let me guess. For a Dr Pepper and free bag of popcorn?" The store offered the popcorn every Tuesday afternoon about this time, but Gordon always needed a soda to wash his down.

"Yes, but that's not what I was going to tell you."

Christa waited for her to continue.

"He finally sold his property out near Dawson's Bend."

"Must've decided to drop the price, huh?"

"I don't know about that. However, it's Crane's Building Supply who bought it."

The smile disappeared from Christa's face and her heart sank. "Are—are you sure?"

"Yes, ma'am. Frankly, I was a little surprised he had the nerve to brag while he was munching on our free popcorn. Hope he chokes on it." Patsy spoke the last words under her breath.

"Now, don't be too hard on him. Gordon's always been a loyal customer."

"So then why'd he go and stab us—you—in the back?" Patsy shook her head.

Christa did feel a little betrayed. Still… "He's been trying to sell that tract for a long time. Perhaps he needs the money."

"Yeah, like I need more kids." The mother of four snorted.

"Well, don't you worry, Patsy. Bliss Hardware has loyal customers. Not to mention relationships with them. People like that." At least she hoped so.

"I expect you're right. I was just a little miffed at the way he told us. Next Tuesday, I'm only filling his popcorn bag half full." With that,

Patsy turned and walked away, leaving Christa wondering if she was too late.

Tomorrow would be two weeks since she'd first contacted her Realtor, and there was still no word from the leasing agent, other than they'd been unable to get in touch with the owner. Perhaps it was time to explore other options. Except there were none. She'd been contemplating this for nearly five months. Ever since she heard Crane's had expressed an interest to a couple of landowners.

The problem was that between the store and the lumberyard, Bliss Hardware was land-locked. And doing away with or decreasing the size of the lumberyard wasn't an option. That would be like shooting herself in the foot. Lumber sales made up the bulk of her business, and every nook and cranny of the store was already packed. That's why the Gebhardt building was the perfect solution.

She blew out a breath. *God, I could really use Your help. Open my eyes to what You would have me do.*

"There you are."

She turned at the sound of Mick's voice to see him striding toward her, his ever-present cowboy hat hin hand.

Forcing a smile, she said, "Well, hello to you, too."

He shoved a hand through his hair. "I have a problem and I was wondering if you might be able to help me out."

Funny, she could have said the same thing to him. That was, if she thought he'd actually be able to help. "Sure, what is it?"

"The probate hearing for Jen's and Kyle's wills has been set for Monday morning."

"That's good."

"Not really. It's at 9:00 a.m. in Austin. That means I need to be on the road before seven. So, I need someone to take Sadie to school. I hate to ask, but—"

She held up a hand. "Don't even go there, Mick. You know I love spending time with Sadie. I'm just glad to know you still trust me with her."

A befuddled look crossed his ruggedly handsome face. "Why wouldn't I?"

This is your chance. Tell him the real reason he needs to stop blaming himself.

She sucked in a breath. "Sadie wouldn't have been outside alone if I hadn't been so fired up about my walls."

His brow puckered. "You know I chose to go with you, right?"

"Still, I was being selfish, pulling you away from her in the first place. I should have waited until she finished playing."

"Christa, you are not selfish. Why would you think such a thing?"

"Because I let you down. You and Sadie. After all you've told me about the Sandersons." Her gaze fell to the dingy linoleum floor. "If they somehow found out Sadie got hurt and used that against you…"

He drew in a deep breath and let it out. "Can't say I haven't thought the same thing a time or two myself. Except I never blamed you."

"I know, because you're too busy blaming yourself." Glancing upward, she saw that hand going through his hair again. It's a wonder the man wasn't bald.

"And to think I was so worried about her falling off of Drifter. Had her wearing that helmet so she wouldn't get hurt. I shoulda gotten a bunch of that Bubble Wrap instead."

"Aisle nine." She pointed, hoping to lighten the mood.

Looking her way, he arched a brow. "Do you think other parents go through this sorta stuff?"

"Probably. But they usually start with infants, so they have a chance to grow with their kids and get their footing. You, well, you got dropped right into the thick of things."

"You're not kidding. And there's no way I would have made it this far without your help." The intensity in his eyes had her swallowing hard.

"Sadie is a precious little girl." Christa was also discovering that her uncle was pretty special, too. A fact she found rather disconcerting. "And I can relate to what she's going through. That's all." She took a step back.

"What do you mean that's all? That's huge. You've helped me understand Sadie in ways I never would have even thought. Sometimes I wonder why Jen thought I could do this."

Forcing herself to look at him, she said, "Because she knew you. She believed in you. And I believe in you, too."

"Now don't go feelin' all sorry for me just because I'm whining."

"Mick Ashford—" her hand automatically went to her hip "—are you calling me a liar?"

"Would you have said what you just did if I wasn't feeling so down?"

"Probably not."

"That's what I—"

"Doesn't mean I wouldn't be thinking it, though." She pretended to straighten the already straight boxes on the shelf. "These past couple of weeks I've gotten to know the real Mick Ashford."

"As opposed to?"

She lifted a shoulder. "A cocky cowboy who thought of me as some crazy broad trying to prove something by buying a hardware store and restoring an old farmhouse."

"First of all, I've never thought of any woman as a 'broad.' Second—" he stepped closer "—I apologize for doubting you. Not only are you smart, you've got more gumption than most men I know."

The sincerity in his voice had her needing to change the subject. "About Monday. I open the store at seven." She reached for another box and sliced it open.

"Oh." He sounded disappointed.

"Why not let Sadie spend the night with me Sunday? That way she can just come to the store with me for a while before I run her to school."

"You sure you want to keep her all night?"

"Why not?" After hearing that Crane's would, in fact, be moving into the area, she could use the distraction. "We'll have fun. We can do a bunch of girlie things."

He shifted from one booted foot to the other, his interest obviously piqued. "Such as?"

She shrugged and tucked the tool away. "Bake cookies, paint our nails, do each other's makeup."

A smile tugged at the corners of his mouth. "Can I be there when y'all make cookies?"

Times like these, she was reminded that Mick

was a big kid himself. "What if they're mermaid cookies with pink and purple sprinkles?"

"I'm pretty sure my taste buds are color-blind."

She couldn't help laughing. Being with Sadie would make for a nice distraction. But Christa still had to come up with a plan. Because if she didn't have a home improvement section up and running well before Crane's opened their doors, she could kiss her business goodbye.

"I can't wait to sleep over at Miss Christa's tonight." Sitting at Mick's kitchen table Sunday morning, Sadie scooped another spoonful of fruity breakfast cereal from her bowl. "We're going to have so much fun."

"I'm sure you will. But we have church first, so eat up." Mick took another swig of his coffee, hoping Christa remembered about the sleepover. He hadn't seen or spoken to her since she'd extended the invitation on Tuesday—something that bothered him more than he cared to admit.

Sadie wasn't the only one who enjoyed spending time with their neighbor. And that left him feeling rather befuddled. Because while no other woman had ever captured his attention the way Christa had, he doubted he could hold hers for very long. The only reason she was a part of his life was because of Sadie. The two of them shared a special bond that had nothing to do with him. And he'd do well to remember that.

His phone vibrated against the table, and his pulse shot up a notch when he saw Christa's name on the screen. Why would she be calling now when it was almost time to head out for morning worship? Maybe she wanted a ride. Or had changed her mind about tonight. That would break Sadie's heart.

"Aren't you going to answer it, Uncle Mickey?"

"Huh? Oh, yeah." He picked up the device and tapped the screen. "Hello?"

"Mick, it's Christa. I think we have a problem."

His gut tightened. She was backing out. He never should have said anything to Sadie. "What's wrong?"

"I'm not sure, but there's a lone cow in the pasture behind my house that doesn't look so good."

He only mildly relaxed. "What do you mean?"

"She's out there all by herself and she just seems…agitated. She lies down for a little bit, then stands up. Her belly is pretty swollen. I think she's pregnant."

Standing, he began to pace. "What does she look like?"

"She's got that mottled brown, black, reddish hide with a white face."

He shoved a hand through his still-damp hair. "Brindle. And yes, she's pregnant. Any idea how long she's been there?"

"Ever since I woke up a few hours ago. Hold on a sec. I'm going to go outside and try to get a closer look."

"Make sure you stay on your side of the fence." The last thing he needed was for Christa to tangle with an ornery, pregnant cow.

"Give me a little credit, Mick." She didn't say anything more, but he could hear the door opening and closing and the sound of birds outside. "All right, let me—ooh, yes, she's definitely pregnant. And I'm pretty sure she's in labor."

"What makes you say that?"

"There are hooves protruding from her—"

"Yeah, I get it." He roughed a hand over his face. "Sounds like she's in distress."

"Which means?"

"That we could lose the calf. Maybe the mama, too." He grabbed his jacket from the hook by the door. "I'm on my way." He ended the call as Sadie finished her cereal. "Put on your boots and jacket, Sadie. We need to check on a cow."

Minutes later, they were in his utility vehicle, making their way up the drive toward Christa's place. Mick prayed nature would take its course and the cow would deliver without any assistance from him. His concern for the cow aside, if he was forced to step in, he didn't know what he'd do with Sadie. He couldn't keep relying on Christa. It wasn't fair to her or Sadie. Besides, it made him long for things that could never be.

Sucking in a deep breath of morning air, he forced himself to calm down as they emerged from the woods and continued toward the farmhouse. The morning sun seemed to be taking advantage of a cloudless sky, threatening to send temps climbing higher than usual this time of year. Then again, Texas weather was just crazy enough to give them an ice storm one month and summertime heat the next.

Despite his concern over the situation, he found himself smiling when he spotted Christa leaning against the back-porch rail, coffee mug in hand as she stared into the pasture, wearing sweatpants and an oversize flannel shirt. She straightened when she saw them, and as they drew closer he noticed the worry that etched her brow.

He brought the UTV to a stop several feet from the porch steps.

Sadie promptly unbuckled her seat belt and hopped out. "Miss Christa!" She hurried up the steps and threw her arms around the woman as Mick continued around the front of the porch for a better look at the cow.

"Good morning," he heard Christa say. "How's the arm?"

"Good. I don't even have to wear my sling anymore."

"That's good to hear."

"Where's Dixie?"

He turned then to see his niece peering up at Christa.

"Inside."

"Can I go see her?"

"You may. However, do not let her outside." Christa's voice was firm. "We don't want her scaring the cow."

Sadie's expression turned serious as she glanced toward the cow, then back to Christa. "I promise."

"All right then."

While Christa opened the door for Sadie, Mick again focused on the cow that lay atop what remained of the hay he'd put out Friday. It had rolled onto its side, but as Mick looked on, it returned to its belly and struggled to stand, its breathing labored. Making it to its feet, it turned, allowing Mick to see the calf's hooves, just as Christa had said. And the cow's udder looked as though it was ready to burst.

Sensing Christa beside him, he said, "Doesn't look like Sadie and I will be going to church today." He met her concerned gaze. "I don't want to intervene with nature unless I absolutely have to, but at the same time, if I wait too long, I could lose both the mama and her calf."

"What are you going to do?" Christa was beside him now.

"Wait. Keep an eye on her. See how she progresses. I may need to call Bum, because if I have to step in, I'm gonna need his help."

"Guess I'd better put on another pot of coffee then."

"Shouldn't you be getting ready for church?"

She puffed out a laugh. "You don't think I'm going to miss watching this calf be born, do you? I mean, I have a vested interest here."

"You do?"

"Not as much as you, but I've been watching her all morning, hoping she'd deliver. I've never had the opportunity to see someone or something give birth before. The closest I came was when Laurel had Sarah-Jane. But even then, I had to leave the room for the delivery."

He couldn't help grinning.

She watched him. "What?"

"You're cute when you get all riled up."

"Stop." Placing a hand on his chest, she gave him a playful shove. "I've been so engrossed in Bessie here that I haven't even showered yet."

He gave her quick once-over, thinking she looked pretty good to him. "You know, I sometimes forget that not everyone has the opportunity to witness life's beginning and end. I can see why you'd be excited."

"Thank you." She took a sip from the cup she still held, though the brew was probably cold by now. "Besides, you can't monitor this cow and keep an eye on Sadie. I'll keep her busy. You just let me know what's happening and when."

Did she have any idea how wonderful she was? She had a knack for reading his mind and anticipating his needs. And then going out of her way to help him. He could get used to that.

Except it wasn't about him. It was Sadie Christa cared about. He was a simple country boy. A rancher with little to offer but his heart. And he'd had that tossed aside enough times to make him quit trying to give it away. So, he'd best pry it off his sleeve and tuck it away. Because Christa was out of his league.

Just then, the cow bellowed.

Mick turned to see it puffing. Time was no longer on his side. Whether he wanted to or not, he had to make a move.

Chapter Ten

So much for distancing.

Christa had done her best to stay away from Mick and Sadie since talking with him at the store Tuesday. And it had been one of the hardest things she'd ever done. Even though she knew she'd be seeing them today, she'd missed them more than she expected, revealing a problem she'd never had before.

She was growing attached. Not only to Sadie, but to Mick. Christa had never met a guy like him. He didn't seek to impress. He was comfortable with who he was and loved what he did. Sure, his new role as a parent had him feeling a little insecure, but he was coming along, and she had no doubt he would continue to strive to be everything Sadie needed him to be.

Right now, though, Christa found herself wishing she hadn't called him about his cow.

Maybe it was the fact that she'd been thrilled to have an excuse to do so. Did she not realize she was putting her heart on the line?

Arms crossed, she trained her gaze on the brindle-colored cow struggling beneath a low-hanging branch of a live oak near the edge of the pasture as Mick called Bum. His deep concern for the cow warmed her and his voice did strange things to her insides. Deep and rich with a country twang that exuded humility and authenticity. Mick was the kind of man she used to dream of, long before reality had jaded her.

Truth was, she wasn't the kind of woman guys wanted to marry. Brody said she was too intimidating. Driven to get her way, no matter the cost. Strange how that had never stopped him from pursuing her and leading her on. Though it did explain why he'd made all sorts of plans for *his* future without ever mentioning them to her until his bags were packed.

"Bum's on his way." Mick dropped his phone into his breast pocket as he addressed her. "I need to run down to my place and get Drifter."

She nodded. "Sadie will be fine here."

"Are you sure?"

She all but glared at him. Why did he keep questioning her when it came to Sadie? "Yes, now go."

Returning to the house, she found Sadie and

Dixie sprawled out on the kitchen floor as Sadie rubbed the dog's belly. Christa put on another pot of coffee and had just pulled a pan of canned cinnamon rolls out of the oven some thirty minutes later when she heard a noise outside.

"What was that?" Beside her, Sadie's eyes were round.

"I don't know. Let's go check it out." Christa turned off the oven. "Dixie, you stay, girl."

Taking hold of Sadie's hand, she led the girl outside where Mick's truck was easing into the pasture, pulling a livestock trailer.

"I thought he was going to get his horse?"

"Drifter's in the trailer." Sadie pointed.

"Hmm." Christa had no idea what was going on. This was a completely new experience for her, as it was for Sadie.

The cow that had been lying down when they first came out stood and stared at the truck. Would she run? Could she?

Movement out of the corner of Christa's eye had her turning to see Bum's green utility vehicle pulling into the drive. He continued alongside Mick's truck as Mick got out.

"What are they going to do?" Sadie clung to Christa as they made their way off the porch.

"Sweetie, I'm afraid I don't know any more than you do. But I think it's best we stay on this side of the fence." Looking down, she saw the girl nodding, her expression filled with wonder.

She understood just how the kid felt. Her own heart was pounding wildly in her chest. The men seemed to be talking forever, and she wished she could be out there to hear what they were saying. With Sadie in her care, though, keeping her safe had to be Christa's first priority.

When Mick moved to the trailer, she noticed he'd changed out of his church clothes. Probably a good move on his part. He opened a door on one side and urged a saddled Drifter out into the pasture. After exchanging a few more words with Bum, he pulled himself into the saddle and gathered a coiled rope in his hands.

Christa couldn't help thinking what a handsome specimen of cowboy Mick made. He was the real deal. Not like those guys whose boots would never see any mud and wore hats that were always pristine.

Mick set his horse into motion, moving in the direction of the cow.

The bovine watched his every move. She did not look happy.

Then Mick began to twirl his lariat until he had a wide loop spinning in the air. The cow tried to make a run for it, but Mick sent the lasso flying, landing it squarely around the cow's neck. He cinched the rope around his saddle horn and waited as Bum repeated the move with a second rope. After a brief battle of wills, the now secured, and probably exhausted, cow relented and lay down.

While Mick remained atop his horse, Bum hopped into Mick's truck and moved the trailer until it was positioned closer to the cow.

Surely they weren't going to move the poor thing while she was in labor.

"I can't see."

Christa lifted Sadie into her arms and continued to watch as the two men attempted to urge the cow to her feet and into the trailer.

"Hold up!" Bum hollered, then motioned for Mick to join him.

Squatting, Mick seemed to study the unborn calf.

Bum moved to the cow's head and grabbed hold of one horn while placing a steadying hand atop her back.

The next thing Christa knew, Mick took ahold of the calf's hooves and pulled it out.

"Yay!" Sadie clapped. "Uncle Mickey gotted the baby."

He got it all right, but from Christa's vantage point, things didn't look good. The calf wasn't moving.

Mick kneeled beside it and vigorously rubbed

the wet, furry body. Moving to the head, he appeared to blow into its nostrils. A few moments passed, then Mick walked away.

Christa's heart twisted. Was it dead? Should Mick have tried harder to save it?

The cowboy motioned for her.

With Sadie still in her arms, Christa made her way along the fence line, out the gate and around to the other side. Drawing closer, her gaze locked on to the unmoving calf. It just lay there, wet and still with its eyes closed.

She swallowed the lump that had formed in her throat and took two more steps.

Suddenly the calf lifted its head as though looking right at her and Sadie.

"It's alive!" The words spilled out as her heart filled with unexpected joy.

"Yes, he is." Mick came alongside them. "It's a bull calf."

"He was so still." She looked up into Mick's weary yet smiling eyes. "I was afraid."

"Yeah, well, he's pretty exhausted."

Christa couldn't help looking at the mama. She lay on her side, her breathing slowly returning to normal. "I think they both are."

"I 'spect she was in labor for quite a while," said Bum.

A pained expression passed over Mick, and Christa had a pretty good idea he was blaming himself. Wondering if he'd ever find the right balance between ranching and caring for Sadie.

"We'll need to move them both down to the barn where I can keep an eye on them. Sometimes when a delivery is tough, a cow will reject the calf."

"What do you do then?"

"Either bottle feed or introduce a nurse cow." He glanced from cow to calf. "I hope she'll accept him."

Christa found herself longing to smooth away the worry lines that creased his brow. "You did a great job."

"Thank you for letting me know. I wasn't aware you paid attention to my cattle."

"Are you kidding? That's one of the things I love most about living in this farmhouse. I get to live on a cattle ranch without having to do any of the work."

That made him smile. "Well, if you'd ever like to pitch in…"

"I might be down for a bottle feeding or two. Should it come to that."

"I want to feed it, too," said Sadie.

"You do?" Mick gathered his niece into his arms.

"Uh-huh." Sadie nodded.

Christa had never seen a more beautiful sight than the dirty, rugged cowboy loving on the precious child left in his care. Despite his tough exterior, Mick had a tender heart. He worked hard and loved deeply. Sadie was blessed to have him.

Christa took a step back. They didn't need her anymore, except as the occasional babysitter, something she was more than happy to do. But her focus needed to be on expanding the store. Growing businesses was her forte, after all. She was driven and independent. The last thing she needed was silly romantic notions getting in her way.

Mick strode down the hallway of the Travis County Courthouse Monday morning, eager to get back to his ranch. He hated the city. Didn't matter which one it was, he wasn't a fan. Throw in the reason he'd had to come in the first place, to get Jen's and Kyle's wills squared away, and well, his day couldn't get much worse. And having Chuck and Belita Sanderson there didn't help. How'd they know he'd be in court today anyway?

Fortunately, the process had been fairly cut-and-dried. Kyle had put most of his and Jen's assets into a trust that now belonged to Sadie, naming Mick as trustee until she was an adult. He would still have to deal with their house, emptying its contents and selling it, but that was a job for another day.

His boots echoed against the shiny tile floor as he continued down the hallway, wondering why on earth Jen had left the old Gebhardt building in downtown Bliss to him instead of Sadie. Granted, the building had been in their family for generations, but he had no interest in it, which was why he'd insisted their mother give it to Jen. She was the one who was all sentimental about the place.

Who knows, maybe I'll want to open a shop in Bliss someday.

He sucked in a breath, knowing he'd give anything to have her here again to do just that.

Perhaps he'd hold on to it for Sadie, along with everything else. Let her decide what she wanted to do with it. In the meantime, he'd settle for enough lease money to cover the taxes. Meaning he should probably contact the leasing agent and find out why it had been empty for so long.

As he approached the exit, he saw the Sandersons standing off to one side, seemingly deep in conversation. To his surprise, they hadn't said a word during the hearing. Now if he could just make it out the door without them noticing him, he'd be home free.

He picked up his pace, taking advantage of his long strides.

"Mick." Chuck's voice crept over Mick's shoulder like a weasel.

Mick thought about making a run for it, but the deputies positioned at the doors would likely think him a criminal.

Slowing his steps, he turned and faced the well-dressed couple as they approached. Chuck wore a navy sports coat over a pale-blue button-down shirt with khaki trousers, while Belita looked the height of fashion in black slacks, heels and a stylish gray sweater topped with an enormous pearl necklace.

Fingers tipped with long nails gracefully brushed Belita's short silver hair to one side as they neared. "Mick, darling, it's so good to see you." The words dripped from her red lips like honey. Make that honey laced with arsenic. The woman couldn't stand him. Thought he was beneath them. A fact she'd made perfectly clear on more than one occasion leading up to the funeral. But here in public, she had to make a good show. Talk about fake.

"Belita." He nodded in her direction first, then her husband's. "Chuck. What are you doing here?"

"Looking out for our granddaughter, of course." Hands shoved in his pockets, Chuck rocked back on the heels of his custom Lucchese boots. "We wanted to make certain everything was handled appropriately."

Like Mick was going to buy that. Chuck had called the judge by his first name and chatted with him about his family, as though they'd known each other forever.

Mick willed himself to remain calm, though. "Kyle put everything in a trust for Sadie. And that's where it's going to stay until she's twenty-one."

"But you are the trustee, dear." Belita's blue eyes had an accusatory look. "And what about their house?"

"Money from the sale of it will also go into the trust fund."

"All of it?" She watched him intently, her false lashes looking like black spiders.

Mick refused to lose his temper, but he was definitely struggling. "Look, I am perfectly capable of providing for Sadie without tapping into Kyle and Jen's money."

"A child means lots of extra expenses," said Chuck. "Things like hospital visits can add up quickly."

Hospital? Surely they didn't know about Sadie's fall.

"How is Sadie's arm doing?"

He glared at the man, wondering how these

two conniving people could have possibly been related to someone as giving and kindhearted as Kyle. "How did you know about that?"

"Where is our granddaughter, anyway?" Belita ignored his question.

"She's at school."

"Surely you had to leave early to get here." The woman fingered her necklace, appearing the picture of innocence.

Still, he refused to give them the satisfaction of knowing they were getting to him. "Yes, ma'am. A good friend of mine took care of her for me."

One perfectly arched brow rose. "This wouldn't be the so-called *friend* who stayed with you at your cabin, would it?"

His right eye twitched as his gaze narrowed. "With all due respect, I'm not sure that's any of your business."

"Sadie is our granddaughter." Chuck puffed his chest out. "That makes it our business."

Yeah, just like everything else.

"Chr—" Catching himself, he cleared his throat. "My friend and Sadie have become quite close."

"Mick—" Belita shifted her oversize leather purse from one elbow to the other "—do you really think it's appropriate to have your lady friends around Sadie?"

"I can assure you there's never been anything inappropriate. Christa isn't a lady friend. She's strictly a friend. Now, if you will excuse me." Fists clenched, he made his way to the exit, kicking himself for revealing Christa's name. And furious with the Sandersons for driving him to it. How did they know about Christa anyway? That she'd stayed at his place? And how did they know about Sadie's arm?

He sucked in a breath of cool air as he stepped outside. Traffic moved past him as he propelled himself toward the parking lot on the next block. Not once in his forty-five years could he recall being this upset.

Had the Sandersons been there today for the sole purpose of irritating him? Because if so, they'd definitely achieved their goal. And it infuriated him that he'd let them do it.

After crossing the street, he located his truck and threw himself inside.

He would never forgive himself if Sadie was forced to live with those wretched people. He couldn't disappoint Jen and Kyle like that. And what about Sadie? Her world would be flipped upside down all over again.

Releasing a guttural sound, he shoved the key in the ignition, feeling as though he might go crazy. He needed to sort through everything that had just happened and calm down. But left to his own devices, that wasn't going to happen. He needed to talk to Christa. She'd been the calm in just about every storm he'd faced lately. And right now, he longed to hear her voice. To hear her tell him that everything was going to be okay. To know that someone had his back.

He pulled the phone from his breast pocket, pressed a few buttons to dial her number, then put his truck into gear.

"Hey, Mick. I was hoping you'd call." Her voice washed over him like a cool rain on a hot summer day, easing his tension. "How did everything go?"

"The hearing was uneventful. The Sandersons were there, though."

"Uh-oh."

He pulled into the busy street. "They were perfectly fine until I was leaving the building. Then they decided to pounce."

"What did they do?"

He told her about the exchange, wishing he'd handled things better. Man, those two knew how to push his buttons.

"I'm sorry, Mick. I wish I could have been there with you. Maybe they wouldn't have messed with you then. I am curious to know how they found out about Sadie's arm and me staying with you. I wonder if they hired a private investigator or something."

"I wouldn't put it past them." A red light had him slowing to a stop behind a line of cars.

"Of course, with folks in Bliss being so friendly, I can see how it wouldn't be too hard to get that kind of information."

"I suppose you're right."

"You know, this reminds me of David and Goliath," she said. "How Goliath was all cocky, demeaning David as he came out to face him. Taunting him."

"And David told the giant that he came in the name of the Lord."

"That's right. Mick, you're not going up against the Sandersons alone. God is with you. No matter what happens, good or bad, God's got this. Your job is simply to trust."

Peace washed over him as the traffic light turned green. "Thank you for that reminder. I needed to hear that."

"We all need to be reminded sometimes. Don't waste your time dwelling on what the Sandersons said. You're a good man, and Sadie is blessed to have you."

"I appreciate that." Not only had she been a godsend, more and more, he was coming to realize that Christa was everything he'd ever wanted in a woman. He just wasn't sure he could ever be enough for her.

She was from the city. Had worked for big

corporations. She was an executive! He couldn't say that about any other woman he'd ever known. Yet they were always trying to change him. Wanting him to be something he wasn't. They always wanted more. More time, more attention, more glamour. They wanted an urban cowboy, not a real cowboy. And that wasn't who he was.

Chapter Eleven

"Christa. Jade Reynolds here."

Sitting at the desk in her office at the store, phone pressed to her ear, Christa couldn't help wondering why her old acquaintance and head-hunter would be calling her.

"Jade. Wow, long time, no hear."

"Too long, if you ask me. However, an opportunity crossed my desk recently that is tailor-made for you. It ticks off every one of your wish-list items, which I still have, by the way. This client wants the best of the best and is willing to pay for it."

Christa eyed the stack of catalogs to her left. "Jade, you know I'm not in the business anymore. I'm quite content owning my little hardware store here in Bliss." Even if her so-called friends had thought her a fool for doing so.

"Sweetheart, do you have any idea what a waste of your talents that is?"

"I don't care. I'm genuinely happy here." And nowhere near as uptight as she'd been in Austin.

A heavy sigh crackled through the line. "If you say so. But if you change your mind, I want to be the first one to know."

Glancing toward the window that overlooked the store, she spotted her friends Paisley and Laurel heading her way, along with Laurel's toddler, Sarah-Jane. "All right, but don't hold your breath, Jade."

Ending the call, she dropped the phone onto her desk and hurried to greet her friends. "Well, hello there." After brief hugs, she relieved Laurel of Sarah-Jane and blew raspberries on her chubby cheeks. "Oh, how I've missed those giggles."

Christa, Laurel, Paisley and Rae, owner of Rae's Fresh Start Café and now Laurel's sister-in-law, had moved to Bliss within a year or so of each other. They'd arrived looking for new beginnings and ended up finding each other.

She settled the almost-two-year-old child on her hip. "What brings you all by?"

"You." Paisley, a tall, gorgeous redhead with a sweet Southern drawl, held a plate of what appeared to be lemon bars. "Where have you been

keeping yourself? We haven't seen or heard from you since the ice storm."

Starting back into her office, she motioned for them to follow. "Well, believe it or not, I've been helping Mick Ashford adjust to fatherhood."

Both women's eyes widened.

"Oh, this definitely calls for some sugar." Paisley peeled back the plastic wrap. "Let me grab a couple of napkins then you can explain." She rounded the corner to the coffeepot, giving a pregnant Laurel just enough time to ease into one of the industrial-style side chairs before returning. "All right, I'm all ears."

While Paisley served up the unexpected treats, Christa settled into her desk chair with Sarah-Jane in her lap. "Mick's sister and brother-in-law were killed in a helicopter crash right after Christmas. Mick is now raising their five-year-old daughter." She explained how things had gotten started with Sadie's bedroom and how she'd ended up having to stay with them during the storm.

A pained expression clouded Laurel's pretty face. "That is so sad. Though I'm grateful Sadie's parents had the forethought to name a guardian. I remember stressing over that before Wes and I were married, wondering what would become of Sarah-Jane if anything were to happen to me."

"That's sweet of you to help Mick navigate the waters of parenthood." Paisley took a bite of a lemon bar.

Picking off a small piece for Sarah-Jane, Christa laughed. "As if I know anything about parenting. However, having lost my mom when I was five, I know what Sadie is going through."

"How does Mick feel about his new role?" Licking her fingers, Laurel eyed Christa intently.

"Scared." The image of him holding Sadie that day the calf was born played across her mind. "But he adores her and is making every effort to be the best father figure he can be." She stood a squirmy Sarah-Jane on the area rug and watched her toddle toward her mother. "He's kind of shattered all the notions I had about him."

"How so?" Laurel scooped her daughter into her arms.

"I always thought of him as a superficial guy. Doing whatever he wanted when he wanted. Only thinking about himself. But now that I've had the opportunity to get to know him, I see how kindhearted he is and realize he's one of those genuinely good guys." She glanced at Laurel. "Like Wes."

Her friends shared a look that Christa knew all too well.

"Oh, stop it. We're friends and that's it."

"I've heard that before." Paisley was obviously referencing a similar claim Laurel had made about Wes.

"Paise…" Christa glared at her friend.

"I'm just saying."

"Well, quit." Christa snagged the last lemon bar. "What's been going on with you two? Laurel, how's baby number two coming along?"

"So far, so good." She set a hand on her slightly swollen abdomen. "Which reminds me, I need to stop by one day when my hands aren't so full—" she eyed Sarah-Jane "—to check out some paint samples for the nursery."

"So will it be a pink or blue nursery?" Christa was eager for an inside scoop.

"Neither. I'm thinking a midrange greige I can accent with any color."

Sarah-Jane started to fuss.

"And on that note, I think we've reached our limit." Laurel stood.

Christa did, too, and moved to hug her friends. "I love you guys."

"We love you, too."

No sooner had they waved goodbye than Christa's phone rang again. Hurrying to her desk, she looked at the device to see her Realtor's name. "Yes!" She swiped the screen.

"Hello." Excitement bubbled inside of her. *Please, let it be good news.*

"Hi, Christa. I'm so sorry this has taken so long, but I finally heard back from the leasing agent and, sadly, the owner does not want to sell. However, if you'd be interested in leasing—"

Her heart dropped. "Leasing won't work for what I want to do. And doesn't the owner realize the building has been sitting empty for at least six months? That's certainly not making them any money."

"I know, but some people are just weird like that. The place probably has sentimental value or something."

Christa heaved a sigh. "All right, thank you for checking." She ended the call, realizing her dream had just gone poof. What was she supposed to do now? That building had been the only viable option for expanding the store.

"Miss Christa!"

She jerked her head up to see Sadie standing in the doorway.

A second later, Mick appeared behind her. "Sorry about that. She ran ahead of me."

"I tolded you, I need to talk to Miss Christa." Sadie had a way of making Christa smile, no matter how bad her mood.

She approached them now. "What's going on?"

"I need to talk to you." Sadie looked from Christa to Mick. *"Alone."*

Mick frowned. "Young lady, this is a workday and Miss Christa owns this store. You need to ask her if she's available to talk."

The child's green eyes swung to her. "Are you abailable?"

Christa couldn't help chuckling. "For you, always."

Sadie sent Mick a look.

"All right, I'll go look at power tools or something." He turned on his booted heel and walked away as Sadie moved into the office.

"How's the calf doing?" Christa perched on one of the side chairs and motioned for Sadie to join her in the next seat.

"I feeded him his bottle this morning."

Bottle? "His mama's having problems with him still?"

"Yeah. She's mean. She kickeded him away."

"Oh, you're right. That isn't very nice. So, what's this important thing you need to talk to me about?"

"I want to have a birthday party for Uncle Mickey." Sadie looked very serious.

"Okay… When is his birthday?"

"Saturday."

"*This* Saturday?" Nothing like short notice. "Are you sure?"

"Yes. I askeded him when his birthday was, and he said Febwary 8. And when I asked my teacher when that was, she said Saturday."

The kid had really put some thought into this. "Where would you like to have this party?"

Sadie shrugged. "I dunno. You have a big house, though. We could have it there."

Hmm… "Who do you want to invite to this party?"

Touching a finger to her chin, Sadie said, "Well… Mr. Bum. And you." Her finger tapped. "Do you know who Uncle Mickey's friends are?"

"I do not. But I'm sure he would enjoy having Mr. Bum there." And it would be good for Bum to get out.

"But we can't have a party with only two people." Sadie sighed and slouched.

"With you and your uncle that's four of us."

"Oh, yeah. 'Cept I want to give him a *big* party." She spread her arms wide. "Because I love him so much and I want him to have the bestest party ever."

Christa had to admire the child's enthusiasm. "Maybe we could invite some of your friends."

Christa narrowed her gaze. "Would you want somebody else's friends at your birthday party?"

Sadie thought for a minute, then grinned. "If they brought presents."

Shaking her head, Christa said, "Tell you what. I'll talk to Mr. Bum and see if he knows anything about Mick's friends."

"Okay but tell them it's a surprise." Sadie clapped her hands together.

"Oh, so it's a surprise party." Way to up the pressure. It had been a long time since Christa had thrown any kind of party. Even then, it was only her, Paisley, Rae and Laurel. But Sadie was so excited, there was no way Christa could turn her down.

"I'll have to come up with a dinner menu." Steak might be good. Ranchers liked steak, she liked steak. And baked potatoes and salad were easy.

"Don't forget the cake." Excitement laced Sadie's voice.

"No, can't forget the cake. Do you know what kind of cake he likes?"

"Chocolate. I askeded him."

"Chocolate cake it is then."

"And I hafta get a present for him."

Standing, Christa faced the child. "You don't think the party is enough of a present?"

"No, silly. You can't unwrap a party."

Christa feigned a face palm. "You're right. What was I thinking? What do you want to get him then?"

"I don't know." Mouth twisted, she looked up at Christa. "Will you help me?"

Once more, Christa found it impossible to say no. "Of course. But we don't have much time." She just hoped she hadn't bitten off more than she could chew. Given the news from the Realtor, though, perhaps this was just the preoccupation she needed to keep her from wallowing in self-pity.

"Looks like you and I are going to be spending a lot of time together this week."

Darkness was descending on the ranch as Mick pulled into Christa's driveway at six fifteen Saturday evening. A sense of relief sifted through him when he saw that the only other vehicle to be found belonged to her. Because while she'd invited him and Sadie, claiming, "Everyone deserves to be treated to a nice birthday meal," a part of him worried that she might be trying to pull one over on him. Sadie had been so insistent about talking to the woman that he feared they might be plotting one of those surprise parties the way Heather had when he'd turned forty.

The memory had him shaking his head. That had been one of the worst nights of his life. Not only had the majority of the guests been her friends, people he barely knew, but Mick hated being the center of attention. The fact that Heather hadn't figured that out after nearly two years of dating was the main reason they'd broken up. Though when he looked back, he realized it had been long overdue.

This time, though, he could relax and be himself.

Retrieving his black felt hat from the center console, he stepped out of the truck dressed in a pair of medium-wash Wranglers with a sharp crease, his favorite black pearl-snap shirt, silver belt buckle and black boots. After closing his door, he moved to the back seat and lifted Sadie to the ground. She'd insisted on wearing a frilly purple dress that hadn't seen the light of day since she'd come to live with him, but still paired it with her pink boots. The kid obviously had her own idea of style.

"Come on, Uncle Mickey." She hurried toward the house, motioning for him to follow.

He caught up with her as she reached the bottom step. "Hold up there, little lady." Taking hold of her hand, they continued toward the door.

He knocked and waited.

"I'm so e'cited," said Sadie.

"Yeah, you love being with Miss Christa, don't you?" He couldn't say that he blamed her.

He liked being with her, too, and wished he had an excuse to see her more often.

After a few seconds, Christa opened the door. A smile curved her pretty lips when she said, "Wow, don't you two look nice."

Not near as nice as she did, and Mick found himself staring. She was wearing the same red dress she'd had on at church that Sunday after the storm. He *really* liked that dress. The color made her eyes sparkle, and the top fit her a lot better than those Bliss Hardware shirts.

He cleared his throat as they moved into the mudroom. "You clean up pretty well yourself, little lady." He knew calling her "little lady" would get a rise out of her.

Sure enough, she lifted a brow. However, the grin that accompanied it told him she knew he was messing with her. "I hope y'all are hungry." She started into the kitchen with Sadie on her heels while he brought up the rear, dropping his hat on a coat hook as he passed.

"Something smells goo—"

"Surprise!"

Mick nearly jumped out of his skin. Then he caught sight of the group of people standing between the kitchen and living room and his insides cringed. *Not again.*

Beside him, Sadie giggled. "Are you surprised, Uncle Mickey?"

"I sure am, princess." He lifted her into his arms, his gaze drifting to Christa. "You did this?"

Christa held up her hands in surrender. "It was Sadie's idea. I was merely her assistant."

"Uh-huh." Sadie nodded. "I wanted you to have the bestest party ever, 'cept I'm too little to do it by myself."

Bum approached and clapped him on the shoulder. "Looks like we got you pretty good."

"You sure did." And Mick didn't know how he felt about it. Then he perused the faces of those who'd gathered.

Johnny Probst and Russell Kemp, his best buddies since kindergarten, were there with their wives, along with his friend and fellow rancher Bobby Wilder and his bride. Folks he knew and loved, yet rarely ever had the opportunity to spend time with because they were all busy with their own lives. Now Christa and Sadie had brought them together.

This just might turn out to be one of the best nights he'd had in a long time.

Over the next few hours, the whole lot of them ate, laughed over dominoes and jabbered until their jaws ached. It had been a long time since he'd seen that old farmhouse filled with so many fond memories. Mick almost hated to see it end. But at a little before eleven, he and Christa waved goodbye to their last guest.

As they made their way back into the kitchen, Mick said, "Let me help you clean up."

"What about Sadie?" Christa gathered up a handful of red plastic cups from the table. "She probably needs to get to bed."

Grabbing several paper plates, he said, "I'm pretty sure she's still crashed on your couch with Dixie right next to her. So, I have plenty of time." He moved beside her to deposit them in the trash. "Thank you for doing all of this." He swept an arm through the kitchen. "I can't begin to tell you how much fun I had tonight."

"Good." She wiped her hands on a dish towel, resting her hip against the counter. "But this party was Sadie's idea."

"True, but you did all the work."

"Your niece can be very persuasive, you know?" She folded the towel and set it aside. "She's too cute for her own good."

"Tell me about it. I don't know what I'm going to do when she's a teenager."

"Wait until she's old enough to date." Christa waggled her eyebrows.

"Oh, way to ruin my birthday, Slocum."

She lifted a shoulder. "I do what I can."

"Well—" taking a step closer, he took hold of her hands, his gaze drifting from her eyes to her lips and back again "—you did a lot. And I'm not just talking about tonight. These last few weeks, you've gone above and beyond for both me and Sadie." He breathed in her sweet fragrance. "Thank you." He lowered his head, his gaze now fixed on her lips.

"Where'd everybody go?" Sadie's sleepy question had Christa taking a giant step back.

Talk about bad timing.

He crossed to his niece and gathered her into his arms. "It's late, princess. We should get you to bed." He sought out Christa then. She was still near the sink, her hands clasped tightly in front of her. "I'm sorry to bail on you. We'll be back first thing in the morning to help you clean up."

Shaking her head, she started toward them. "That's all right. Johnny and Russell's wives already helped me with the bulk of it." She smoothed a hand over Sadie's back. "You gave your Uncle Mickey an awesome party tonight." Pushing up on her tiptoes, she kissed his niece's cheek. "Sleep well, Sadie."

Regret twisted his stomach as he headed out the door, down the steps and all the way to his truck. He didn't want to leave. He wanted to be back there in Christa's kitchen, knowing, not wondering, how she felt in his arms. The taste of her lips.

Yeah, if he had any doubts about his feelings for Christa, tonight had eradicated all of them. Like it or not, he'd fallen for her. Question was, how did she feel about him?

Chapter Twelve

Mick had almost kissed her. And Christa had wanted him to.

That had been Saturday night. Now it was Wednesday, and she hadn't talked to him since. Then again, she'd purposely been avoiding him. Didn't even respond when he called to thank her again for the party. There was no point. The party that had managed to distract her from her problems for a few days was over. It was time to focus on other things. Like her business.

Her only hope for expansion—at least the only logical one—had been a bust, so now she was facing the impending arrival of Crane's without even the slightest clue as to what to do next.

With the aid of a pallet jack, she maneuvered a load of base paint down aisle two. She'd never been one to panic. After all, she knew God was

in charge and if He closed the door on the Gebhardt building, He would open a door somewhere else. She just wished she knew where
that door was and when it would open.

*An opportunity crossed my desk recently that
is tailor-made for you.* Jade's phone call played
across her mind.

Surely God wasn't calling Christa back to the
corporate world. A shiver ran through her. No,
that wouldn't— *It ticks off every one of your
wish-list items.*

That wish list had to be five years old. Her
life was different now. *She* was different now.

No, she could never go back to corporate life
where it was all about looking out for number
one. She'd put her own desires before God and
her father for far too long, and that wasn't going
to work anymore. If God wanted her to take
that job, He was going to have to speak loud
and clear.

She positioned the pallet in front of the paint
counter, removed the jack and wheeled it to the
back room, well aware that she needed to continue to be proactive when it came to expanding
Bliss Hardware. Because sitting around waiting
for something to drop out of the sky wasn't right
either. It was important to be a good steward of
what God had given her and, by prayer and sup-
plication, she would make her desires known to

Him every step of the way, trusting that He had a plan for her and her dreams.

Yet as she parked the pallet jack and looked around her store, which seemed to be bulging at the seams, the urge to drop to her knees and plead with God to make that door be to the Gebhardt building nearly overwhelmed her. It was the only option that made sense. Unfortunately, it wasn't an option anymore.

Returning to the pallet of paint, she sliced through the shrink-wrap with her utility knife and peeled it away, images of Mick once again playing across her mind. As much as she hated to admit it, she missed spending time with him and Sadie. But after what happened the other night, things just felt…weird. The awkwardness of not knowing how he felt about her had her wondering how she should even act around him now. While she'd grown to care deeply for both Mick and his niece, what purpose would it serve in the end if he didn't return those feelings? She wasn't sure she'd be content to remain friends, knowing that she wanted more.

She gathered two gallons of paint in each hand and moved onto aisle three, where she lined them up on the proper shelf with the labels facing forward. She didn't want one of her employees accidentally grabbing a deep base satin when what they really needed was a light base semigloss.

"Did you hear Crane's Building Supply is fixin' to build out past Gordon Winslow's old place?"

Christa's heart skidded to a stop as she listened to the man on the next aisle.

"Sure will be nice not having to drive all the way into the city for all that stuff my wife keeps wantin' 'round the house," a second man said.

"Yeah, we'll have one-stop shopping right here in the county."

The proverbial knife that felt as though it'd been plunged into her heart twisted. If what they were saying was true, people were already looking to Crane's to meet their needs, amplifying her desire to expand now so by the time Crane's opened, folks would already think of Bliss Hardware as their go-to home improvement store. She wanted Bliss Hardware to be their first thought, not an afterthought.

A mixture of anger and hurt had her abandoning the paint and propelling herself across the store with determined steps. Her heart ached and she wanted to scream. She needed some fresh air to clear her mind before she completely lost it.

Throwing open the back door, she continued outside—and ran right into Mick.

"Whoa there." He placed a strong, steadying hand on each of her shoulders. "Christa?" Easing his grip, he lowered his head to meet her gaze, concern narrowing his light green eyes. "What's wrong?"

In that moment, the desire to have someone to lean on was stronger than ever. It would be so easy to fall into his muscular embrace. To savor his presence and draw from his strength. And if they weren't at the store, she just might have given in. But the smell of lumber drifting on the breeze reminded her of where she was.

Straightening, she took a step back and reined in her thoughts. She wasn't used to sharing her burdens with anyone but God, and she wasn't about to start now. The last thing she needed was Mick feeling sorry for her.

The midafternoon air seemed warmer than usual as she drew in a calming breath. "Sorry about that. I'm fine. Really."

"You sure?" He adjusted his cowboy hat. "Because for a second there you looked madder'n an old wet hen."

A train horn sounded in the distance. Before long, it would be barreling right past them, making conversation impossible. But not soon enough.

She brushed the hair away from her face and squared her shoulders. "Yes, I'm sure." Shoving her hands into the pockets of her jeans, she looked everywhere but at Mick. "What are you doing here?"

"I needed T posts. I've got some fences that need shoring up, and I'd rather knock 'em out while the temperatures are still relatively cool."

"I can certainly understand that." Nobody wanted to be working fence lines in July. "How's Sadie?" She managed a glance in his direction.

"Fine." A forklift rumbled through the lumberyard as he continued to watch her. It was starting to make her uncomfortable. "Sorry, but I gotta ask this again. Are you sure you're all right? You seem, I don't know—frustrated."

Of course she was frustrated. The business she'd worked so hard to build was in danger of going under. Another small business falling prey to corporate giants.

And having Mick so close when she'd been thinking about that almost-kiss wasn't helping either.

"I've just got a lot on my mind, that's all."

"Okay. But if you need to talk, you know I'm here for you, right?"

She nodded, wishing she could turn to him. But she knew better than to rely on someone else. Especially someone who had the capability to break her heart. She needed to keep Mick at arm's length. Because if she let him in the way she'd done with Brody, her heart would definitely end up broken. And this time, she might not survive.

"This is terrible." Sadie dropped her head into her little hands late Thursday afternoon.

"What if we put some more glitter on it?" Mick picked up the shaker container, fearing his kitchen table would be sparkly from now on.

Sadie looked from the partially decorated shoebox to the stickers, markers and construction paper that littered the table and heaved a dramatic sigh. "It's just not working."

He couldn't help but chuckle. She sounded so much like her mother. Jen had always wanted things just so. She was all about presentation. Gifts had always been beautifully wrapped; her house looked like it belonged in a magazine...

He scanned his brown and green living space. Obviously, Sadie had inherited her mother's genes.

"What do you think it needs?" He didn't particularly want to make another run to the store, but he would if he needed to. Then he'd make a list, so he'd know what to get next year.

"I dunno." Another sigh. A second later, she straightened. "Maybe Miss Christa could help me."

Mick's insides knotted. He couldn't call Christa.

Ever since their near kiss, things had been different. He got the feeling she didn't even want to be around him anymore. Served him right for trying to kiss her. He knew she was too good for him, yet for a moment he'd allowed himself to believe he might stand a chance.

Boy was he wrong. When he'd seen her at Bliss Hardware the other day, she couldn't seem to get away from him fast enough.

"Sadie, I don't think we should keep bothering Miss Christa."

"Please?" Her bottom lip pooched out.

He felt himself caving faster than a house of cards. Would he ever grow immune to the pouting?

"All right, I'll check with her. But if she says no, we'll have to figure this out on our own, okay?"

"Okay." *Now she smiles.*

He rolled his eyes, the knot tightening in his gut as he dialed Christa. She might not even answer once she realized it was him.

Moving to the window, he stared out over the cow pond. The sight usually calmed him.

"Hello?"

He whirled back around. "Christa, hey, it's Mick." As if she couldn't read the caller ID. "Sadie is in the process of decorating a shoebox for her Valentine's party at school tomorrow and, well, she's having a problem."

"What kind of problem?"

"An inept uncle, for starters."

No response.

"Christa?"

"I'm here. I just…" Another pause. "What materials does she have to work with?"

Eyeing the table again, he rattled them off.

"Got it. Has she done her valentines yet?"

"No, she was pretty eager to get the box done."

"Well, tell her to work on the valentines now and then Dixie and I will drop by just as soon as I get off work."

Part of him relaxed while another part grew more nervous. "You're a lifesaver. Thank you."

Well, that went better than he thought it would. Except for all the hesitations. Was she busy, or did she not want to be bothered?

He passed Christa's instructions on to Sadie, then breathed a sigh of relief when she happily went to work filling out her valentines.

An hour and fifteen minutes later, there was a knock at the door. Sooner than he'd expected. Sadie had just finished her valentines, and the aroma of frozen pizzas baking in the oven drifted through the house as he opened the door.

Christa's dog sashayed in first, seemingly looking for Sadie.

"Dixie!" Sadie jumped out of her seat as the golden trotted her way. "I misseded you so much." She hugged and kissed the animal.

Mick looked at Christa, who was holding a small sack. "Once again, I find myself indebted to you. Can I start by offering you some pizza? It's just about to come out of the oven."

"So that's what's making my stomach growl. I would love some."

After they'd polished off both the cheese and supreme pizzas, Christa sat down at the table with Sadie and examined her valentine's box. "This is a great start. I think it just needs a few more elements."

"What are elemems?"

"Elements," Christa gently corrected. "All it means is that it needs more stuff."

"Oh." Sadie appeared worried as she looked over the items Mick had bought her. "But this is all I have."

"That's what your uncle said. So I brought a few more items." She retrieved her bag from the side chair and pulled out things one by one. "I've got some iridescent ribbon."

Sadie gasped excitedly.

"Some pink and red foam sheets we can cut into shapes to add dimension. *And*—" she grinned at Sadie "—some boas." She removed a conglomeration of red and white feathers before setting the bag aside. "What do you think?"

"I'm going to have the bestest valentimes box ever!"

Mick pulled up a chair and watched the two as they worked. Christa was so good with Sadie, guiding and teaching her, and Sadie soaked up the attention like a dried-out sponge. In no time they had the sides of the red-glitter-coated box wrapped in a pink boa, and they'd added a shimmery bow to the top. Now Christa was cutting out bright pink letters that spelled Sadie's name.

"We'll put these on the top so everyone will know this is *your* box," Christa said.

When they'd finished, Sadie was so proud, Mick had to take a picture of the two showing off their work of art.

Christa was gathering up her things when Sadie hugged her around the waist.

"I'm so glad you helpeded me." She peered up at the woman. "I'm sorry if I bovered you."

Christa looked surprised. "Sadie, you are never a bother. Why would you think that?"

"Uncle Mickey said we shouldn't bover you."

"I see." Christa's gaze cut to Mick. "Next time you'll have to remind your Uncle Mickey that I *like* spending time with you. *Both* of you."

She turned her attention back to Sadie. "Now I want you to have the bestest Valentine's party ever, okay?"

"Okay."

"Come on, Dixie." Christa started toward the door.

"I'll walk you out." Mick looked at his niece. "Sadie, it's getting late. I want you to get your pajamas on and brush your teeth. I'll be right back."

He followed Christa and her dog onto the porch, feeling a bit uncertain, but determined to push forward anyway.

Shoving his hands into the pockets of his jeans, he said, "You, uh, said you like spending time with *both* Sadie and I." He shrugged. "Is that just on occasion or a regular basis?"

Now it was her turn to look nervous. And that suited him just fine. "I've grown fond of you both."

He dared a step closer. "Can I just be honest here?"

"Please."

"I like you." He shoved a frustrated hand through his hair. He sounded like some bumbling teenager. "And I don't know if it's just me, but I can't help wondering if this—" he waved a hand between them "—could be something more than friendship."

She licked her lips. Rocked back on her heels. And stared toward the barn for the longest time. "No. It's not just you."

"That's a relief." He couldn't help but smile when she finally met his gaze. "I'm not sure where to go from here, though."

Something flickered in her hazel eyes. "Well, we could start by picking up where we left off Saturday night at my place. You know—" she tilted her head "—before Sadie woke up."

Under the light of a full moon, his heart pounded as he closed the distance between them. He cupped her face in his hands, his thumbs caressing the soft skin of her cheeks. She was so beautiful. And she liked him, simple cowboy that he was.

Lowering his head, he claimed her sweet lips, allowing his fingers to thread into her soft waves. Her hair smelled like apples. He inhaled deeper, longing to get lost in her. She was as refreshing as an autumn day after a long, hot summer. And she was in his arms.

When he finally pulled away, he tucked her head beneath his chin and held her, savoring the feel of her. He didn't want this moment to end. But Sadie was waiting on him.

He released his hold, lowering his hands until his fingers entwined with hers. "I reckon I should go check on Sadie."

"Yes, you should." Her cheeks were pink as she smiled up at him. "We can talk later."

Nodding, he started to let her go, then tightened his grip. "I promised Sadie we'd do a campfire Saturday night. Care to join us?"

Her eyes sparkled. "Sounds like fun. I'll bring stuff for s'mores."

"No need. I've already got them."

"In that case—" she leaned toward him and pressed a brief kiss to his lips "—I'll see you then."

Mick watched her drive away before heading back inside. Whatever was going on inside him was something completely new and different from anything he'd ever experienced before. It scared him to death, while filling him with more happiness than he'd ever imagined.

God, whatever You're up to here, please don't let me blow it.

Chapter Thirteen

❧

Christa never dreamed a kiss could give her so much clarity. Yet as she'd driven away from Mick's last night, she knew just what she needed to do regarding the expansion of Bliss Hardware. And after sleeping on it, she'd headed into the store early, shut herself in her office and had been crunching numbers ever since, until she came up with just how much she was willing to offer for the Gebhardt building.

After moping all of Wednesday, it had occurred to her yesterday that rather than simply stating her desire to purchase the building next door, she needed to make an offer. An actual dollar amount to show the owner she wasn't trying to get something for nothing, but that she was serious. Because people could talk the talk all day long without actually making a move.

Well, she intended to make a move all right,

by making the best offer possible. She wanted to dangle a nice big carrot that would make it nearly impossible for the owner to say no.

Confident with her numbers, she picked up her phone and dialed her real estate agent.

"I know the owner said they're not interested in selling," she told Greta Herne, "but I would like to make them an offer I'm hoping will change their mind." She named her figure.

"Christa, you are not only a determined woman, but a very wise one. After all, they don't say 'money talks' for nothing. I've seen sellers decline one offer, only to have them jump on a better one. Everyone has their price."

"Yes, they do. And I'm hoping this will have the owner of the Gebhardt building jumping."

"So do I, Christa. I'll contact the leasing agent and let you know just as soon as I hear something."

"Great. Thanks, Greta."

With that out of the way, she took a deep, cleansing breath and was about to go check on a lumber shipment when her phone rang. Surely Greta didn't know anything yet.

But when she looked at the screen, it was Jade's name that had her cringing. Why was she calling again?

"Hello."

"Christa, my favorite person." Jade only said

that when she wanted something. "Happy Valentine's Day."

"Sure…same to you."

"So, you know that position I told you about?"

"You mean the one I said I wasn't interested in?"

"That's the one. Except I'm pretty sure your interest will be piqued once you hear what I'm about to tell you."

"Doubtful but go ahead."

"I told them all about you."

"Why? I said no."

"Because I wanted them to know that you are the cream of the crop. And, as a result of that, they would like to extend a second offer to you."

Christa's jaw dropped when Jade rattled off some exorbitant amount. "Nobody's worth that much."

"Well, they seem to think you are."

"They haven't even met me."

"They know a good thing when they see it."

"Jade, I may be good, but I'm definitely *not* interested. No matter how much they offer." She listened to the woman whine until she saw Mick walk into the store. "Sorry, Jade, I have to go."

She tucked her phone away and yanked her office door open as Mick approached, holding a heart-shaped box in one hand and a bouquet of red roses sprinkled with baby's breath in the other.

Her heart skipped a beat. She'd never put much stock into Valentine's Day before. At least, not as an adult. But her time with Mick last night seemed to unlock something inside her—a desire she'd suppressed for so long. She'd convinced herself that she wasn't interested in love or marriage or a family.

Over these past few weeks, she'd found it harder and harder to ignore those longings, though. It seemed the more time she spent with Mick and Sadie, the more desirable those things became, punching holes in the wall she'd built around her heart. And last night had made one thing very clear. Her feelings for Mick had drifted into deeper waters.

Oh, she'd tried to convince herself that they were only an extension of the deep affection she felt for Sadie, but the moment his lips touched hers, the lie she'd been clinging to was blown away, unleashing a truth she could no longer deny. No matter how much it terrified her.

Her excitement spilled over into a goofy grin as the handsome cowboy stopped in front of her. "Good morning."

His smile seemed a bit nervous. Then he shrugged and said, "I couldn't decide, so I got you both."

"And I love them both." She accepted the gifts, inhaling the fragrant flowers while tucking the box of chocolate under her arm. "Thank you."

His expression was unusually shy, so she motioned him into her office. "I won't be sharing these flowers with you—" she set them aside before peeling the plastic wrapping off the box "—however, I think we should both sample the chocolate." She lifted the lid and the enticing aroma made her mouth water. "Take your pick." She held the box up.

With a gleam in his eye, he selected a dark chocolate truffle. "You're in a mighty good mood this morning."

In large part because of the kiss they'd shared last night. But she wasn't about to say that.

She felt her cheeks heat. "I am. I've got flowers and chocolate. Of course I'm happy." She took a bite of a caramel pecan cluster. "And I decided to step out in faith on something that's been bothering me for a while now."

He lifted a brow. "And what's that?"

"I'd rather wait until I have something concrete to share. But when I do, I promise you'll be the first to know."

"I see how it is. One kiss and the secrets begin."

She grabbed another chocolate. "Oh, stop. That's not how it is, and you know it."

"Yeah, I'm just teasing." He reached for her hand. "But if it's anything you need to talk about, I'm here."

Warmth started in her belly and spread throughout her entire body. Mick was someone she could talk to. Someone she could count on to be there for her through thick or thin.

"Since it's Valentine's Day, I thought about taking you out to dinner tonight. But because it's Valentine's Day, every place in town is apt to be crowded."

"Yes, all three of them." She laughed.

"So, I thought I would offer to fix you dinner instead. What do you say? Steaks at my place?"

She winced. "Can I take a rain check?"

"Sure. Is something wrong?"

"No, it's just that Rae, Paisley and I have standing plans. Every year, Paisley treats us to some over-the-top dinner at her place. Laurel used to join us as well, but then she up and got married, so it's just the three of us now."

"How dare she?"

"I know, right?"

His phone buzzed and he pulled it out of his pocket. "It's Cole." He set the device to his ear. "Hello?"

"I'll be right back." Christa grabbed the large

mason jar from atop one of the file cabinets behind her desk and went to the restroom to fill it with water for the flowers. When she returned, Mick was no longer on the phone, but he looked distressed.

"What's wrong?" She set the jar on her desk.

"They've set a date for Sadie's custody hearing."

Her smile evaporated. "When is it?"

"Two weeks from yesterday."

"Where?"

"Here in Bliss. It has to take place in the county where the child resides."

"That's good. Still, I can't believe they got it so quick. I thought it would take a few months." Christa could tell Mick was struggling. She knew better than anyone how much he adored Sadie. And Sadie adored him right back. It made her sick to think of the two of them being torn apart. All because the Sandersons were self-absorbed jerks who refused to consider what was best for their granddaughter.

Reaching for his hand, she gave it a squeeze. "You've got this, Mick. I have to believe that."

"I want to believe it, too. But right now, it's kinda hard."

She squeezed tighter. "Then I'm just going to have to have enough faith for both of us, because we will not allow them to get their hands on Sadie without a fight."

Already down and out after learning about the custody hearing, Mick didn't need another burden to bear. But that didn't stop the real estate person Jen used for the Gebhardt building from dropping a major dilemma in his lap. One that had him debating with himself all night long. Good thing Christa already had plans, because he wouldn't have been very good company.

Somebody must really want to get their hands on the building that had once been home to his great-grandparents' general store, because the offer they'd made had really given him pause. It was enough to put Sadie through a top-notch college and buy her a fancy car without ever having to touch her inheritance.

Yet every time he picked up the phone to call the woman back and say yes, Jen's voice would play through his head. *It's part of our heritage, Mick. And I want Sadie to be able to share in that.*

Strange how she hadn't felt that way about the old farmhouse they grew up in. Instead, she thought it as much of an albatross as he did. So, what was the attachment to the building? And why hadn't she just put it in the trust for Sadie? That would have made his decision a lot easier.

That was, unless Jen thought Mick needed the money. If so, she'd been way off base. He'd ended up contacting the agent Saturday morning to turn down the offer. If Jen loved the building, then he'd hold on to it until Sadie was old enough to decide whether she wanted it or not.

Once that weight was off his shoulders, though, things started looking up. He figured it was either by the grace of God or the fact that Christa would be joining him and Sadie for their campfire tonight. Probably both.

If he would have known that opening up to Christa about his feelings for her would turn out so well, he would have said something a long time ago, instead of second-guessing himself. But knowing that she felt the same way about him lifted his spirits and gave him hope for their future. He could hardly wait to see her tonight.

"All right, Sadie, let's see if we've got everything." Standing in his kitchen just before five, he looked over his list. "Hot dogs and buns?"

"Uh-huh."

"Chips?"

"Yes."

"S'mores stuff? Graham crackers, marshmallows and chocolate bars?"

"Yummy. Yep."

"Ketchup and mustard and hot cocoa mix?"

"And na'kins and cups and spoons."

"Then I think we're ready to go."

When Christa's SUV rolled up an hour later, the campfire was blazing and he'd set up a table that held all of their supplies, including roasting forks and a thermos of hot water. Temperatures had already fallen into the forties, so the cocoa would probably be in high demand.

"She's here!" Sadie cheered and bounded toward the vehicle.

Mick knew just how she felt. He glanced toward a cloudless sky, sending up a prayer of thanks. Should be a great night for stargazing. That was, if he could tear his gaze away from Christa.

She emerged from her vehicle wearing a puffy red jacket, then let Dixie out of the back seat before Sadie practically dragged Christa toward the fire. "We've got hot dogs and s'mores."

Mick met them halfway. "Glad you could make it."

"Me, too." Then how come her smile didn't quite reach her eyes? Was she tired maybe?

He took a step closer, dipping his head for a better look. "You okay?"

Waving him off, she said, "Yeah, just a long day." She sucked in a breath. "So, where's the hot cocoa?"

Mick was pleased to see her mood improve over the next couple of hours. Whether it was because of the food or the company, he couldn't say. But he sure was happy she was here. She fit into his life like no other woman ever had. Accepting him for who he was and capturing his heart along the way.

With his camp chair tucked next to hers beside the fire, they stared at the sky, listening to the sounds of nature and the crackling of the flames.

"This is so peaceful." Christa's voice was soft. "I wish I could stay right here forever."

He'd be okay with that.

Suddenly she gasped. "Look! A shooting star."

"I see it. Sadie, look up."

When his niece didn't respond, he glanced around Christa to find Sadie asleep on the bench.

"Oh, poor baby is tuckered out." Christa moved beside her.

Mick did, too. "Yeah, she had a long day." She didn't even move when he scooped her into his arms. "I'd best put her to bed."

"I can help."

Inside, Christa eased off Sadie's boots and coat before turning down her bed.

Mick settled his niece onto the sheets, pulled

the covers over her and kissed her cheek. "Sleep well, princess." He followed Christa out of the room and downstairs.

When he continued to the door, she said, "Are you sure? I mean, what if she wakes up?"

He loved how she always thought about Sadie. "We're not that far away. Besides, I have this." He retrieved a small video monitor from the shelf beside the door.

"A baby monitor? Isn't she a little old for that?"

"I prefer to think of it as a rancher's helper. That way if I have to be in the barn or something while she's asleep, I can still keep an eye on her."

"Good idea."

Returning to the fire, he said, "You know, there's something I've been thinking about all day."

She paused in front of her chair. "What's that?"

"This." He slipped an arm around her waist, tugged her closer and kissed her.

When they parted, she looked up at him, her eyes bright in the moonlight. "I like the way you think, cowboy."

Grinning, he pulled her to her seat before relaxing in the chair beside her. The fire popped and sizzled, sending sparks dancing into the air as they sat quietly.

Mick wasn't sure he'd ever felt so at peace, and as he looked up at the stars, he couldn't help but thank God for bringing Christa into his life. He tilted his head to look at her. "I don't think I've ever asked you how you ended up in Bliss."

"Well…" Nestling into her seat, she stared into the fire. "After my dad passed away, I was going through his things and came across a magazine with the pages folded back. When I looked at it, there was an advertisement for Bliss, Texas. 'Because everyone needs a little Bliss in their lives,' it had said."

"That's our motto."

She chuckled. "I know. And there was something about it that wouldn't let me go. So two days later, I came to check things out. I don't know if it was the magnolia trees in bloom on the courthouse square, the Victorian buildings or the pride folks had in their town, but I was enthralled." She shrugged. "Then I saw the For Sale sign in the window of the hardware store and knew it was meant to be."

"And just look at how the store has grown since you took it over."

"I know." She frowned. "But it could be so much more."

"What do you mean?"

She hesitated a moment. Buried her hands in the pockets of her jacket and took a big breath. "I want to expand Bliss Hardware and add a home improvement section. And for months I've been racking my brain trying to figure out just how to do that. I mean, the store is landlocked, so adding on is out of the question. Then it hit me that the empty building next door would be perfect."

His chest tightened. "You mean the Gebhardt building?" He swallowed hard.

"Yes. They share a common wall, so all I'd have to do is take out a portion of the brick, shore it up with a frame, and I'd be good to go. The owner doesn't want to sell, though, which I absolutely do not understand. I mean, in the past three years that space has housed a pizza place, a gift shop and a dress boutique. None of which remained open longer than six months. I don't see how that can even cover insurance."

So, she was the unknown buyer. And he was the one who'd shattered her dream.

All of a sudden, he felt sick to his stomach. He had to tell her. But how?

"Maybe it's not about the money. Maybe it has sentimental value." He shrugged, feeling completely torn. He wanted to help Christa, to make her dream a reality. But he was determined to hold on to the building for Sadie, and he wasn't sure he was willing to go back on that. "Have you considered renting?"

"I can't very well tear out that brick wall if I do that."

Lord, help me here. Give me some sort of brilliant idea that might help her.

"You could have a separate store. You know, Bliss Hardware Design Center or something. Make it look nice and homey. Have one of those little awning things out front that makes it seem kind of fancy." The words seemed to tumble out faster than he could think them. And probably didn't make a lick of sense.

"I don't know." Heaving a sigh, she stood. "I'm sorry. I let myself get all worked up and kind of ruined the mood here." She reached for his hand. "I think I'd better call it a night."

Mick had never found himself in such a quandary. He knew he should tell her the truth, but he couldn't seem to find the right words. Not that words had ever been his forte. Still, he owed her truth. Maybe she'd be able to understand why he couldn't sell the building. Or he'd end up ruining the best thing he'd ever found.

"Will I see you tomorrow?"

Her smile was forced. All because of him. "At church. However, Laurel invited me to join her, Wes and Sarah-Jane for lunch." She sighed. "Since I haven't had much time with Sarah-Jane lately, I plan to take full advantage of all the snuggles I can get. Besides, I promised to help Laurel with ideas for her nursery."

"Okay, well…"

A voice inside urged him to tell her now. But he needed to think things through first. Otherwise, he'd bumble his way through any sort of explanation and probably dig himself a hole he might never find his way out of.

Placing her hands against his chest, she pushed up on her toes and brushed a kiss to his lips. "Thank you for a wonderful night. I hope we can do it again soon."

He did, too. But if he didn't tell her the truth— "Christa?" He cupped her elbows as she lowered herself.

"Yes?"

"I—" The words tangled on the tip of his tongue. If he told her now, he'd only make a bigger mess of things. He needed to sleep on it. Sort through his thoughts. "Sleep well."

Chapter Fourteen

Most Sundays Mick enjoyed Pastor Kleinschmidt's messages, but this morning's sermon seemed to go on forever. And sitting beside Christa, Mick felt as though there was a noose tightening around his neck. Sleep had evaded him most of the night, and he knew he wouldn't be at peace until he told her that he was the owner of the Gebhardt building. He could only pray she wouldn't be angry with him for not being forthcoming last night.

When the final chords of the doxology ended, Mick turned to Christa as she gathered up her purse. She looked amazing in a floral-patterned pale blue blouse, dark wash skinny jeans and a pair of those heeled booties that all the women seemed to be into lately.

"When you're done at Laurel's would you

mind giving me a call? There's something I need to talk to you about."

She looked at him, her brow puckering. "Sure. Is everything all right?"

"Yeah." Or would be, just as soon as he told her. At least, he hoped so.

"Okay. I'll call you when I get home."

"Have fun with Laurel and Sarah-Jane."

"I'm sure I will."

As she walked away, Mick felt a hand clamp down on his shoulder. Turning, he saw Bum grinning from ear to ear.

"The two of you sittin' together has become a habit."

Mick just hoped this wasn't the last time.

"You don't look too happy, son. Did Christa send you packin'?"

Not yet. "She's going to Laurel's for the afternoon."

"I see. Well, why don't you and that young'un of yours come join me for lunch? I've got a roast in the slow cooker with some potatoes and carrots. There's more than enough."

Comfort food. Mick could use some comfort about now. Not to mention a friendly ear. Perhaps Bum could help him get things straight in his mind before he talked to Christa.

"All right. Let me gather up Sadie and we'll see you in a bit."

"I haven't been to Mr. Bum's house before." Sadie looked left then right as they made their way up Bum's long drive a short time later. "He's got cows just like you."

Mick couldn't help grinning. "He sure does." He eased his truck around the circle drive before coming to a stop in front of the 1970s-era brick ranch-style house. He climbed out first, then helped Sadie while Bum waited at the door.

"Thank you for 'viting us, Mr. Bum." Standing on the porch, Sadie peered up at the older man.

"It's a pleasure to have you here, young lady."

She took hold of Mick's hand as they walked into the house, obviously feeling a little on the shy side.

"Oh, look out there," Bum said as a miniature brown-and-white fur ball barreled past them. "Sassy, you be careful 'round that little one."

Sadie giggled as she moved in a circle, trying to keep track of the shih tzu that had belonged to Bum's wife, Dorothy. Finally the dog dropped in front of Sadie, seemingly smiling up at her while it wagged its curly tail.

Sadie promptly dropped onto the tile floor. "Aw, it's *so* cute."

Sassy must have taken that as her cue because she pounced into Sadie's lap and began licking her.

"Let her alone, Sassy." Bum shooed the dog away. "You can play with her after we eat." He eyed Mick then. "Food's ready, so y'all come on in the kitchen."

The meal was as tasty as it was hearty, rounded out with some of those crescent-shaped rolls from a can and peach cobbler from Rae's Fresh Start Café.

"Can I play with Sassy now?" Sadie scooted out of the wooden captain's chair a short time later.

Mick eyed her empty plate. "If it's okay with Mr. Bum."

Her green eyes moved to the older man.

"You sure can. She's got a basket of toys right around the corner. And she loves to play ball."

"Careful with the ball, though," Mick was quick to add. "Roll it so you don't risk breaking anything."

As she hurried away, Bum said, "She'll be all right. There ain't nothing she can hurt." Fork in hand, he scooped up another bite of cobbler. "You seem a little somber. Is it the lawsuit?"

"Not this time. This has to do with Christa."

"I would think all this time you've been spending with her would put a smile on your face."

"Normally, it does. But I've gotten myself into quite a pickle."

"How so?"

Mick took a sip of his iced tea before revealing Christa's desire to purchase the Gebhardt building, his refusal to sell and his silence when he found out she was the one wanting to buy it. "I'm standing in the way of her dream. But at the same time, I'm not sure I should let the building go."

"Christa's a smart woman. Just explain that to her." Bum wiped his mouth with a paper napkin. "You know what they say. Honesty is the best policy."

"Yeah, I probably should have exercised that last night, but I was so blindsided I didn't say a word. And I'm afraid that might come back to bite me."

"Then I'd suggest you rectify things just as quick as you can." Bum belched under his breath.

"That's what I intend to do. I told her to call me when she got home."

"Good." The older man massaged the area beneath his breastbone, his expression suddenly pinched.

"You okay?"

"Yeah. This heartburn's really been getting to me lately." He picked up his plate. "Reckon I need some more of those antacid tablets." When he stood, Mick noticed his friend was looking a little gray. And he was sweating.

"Maybe you should go lie down."

"Nah, I'll be—" A look of panic lit Bum's eyes. He thrust the plate toward the counter. It landed with a crash as Bum clutched his chest.

"Bum!" Mick bolted from his chair and caught the man before he hit the floor. Easing him onto the tile, he looked down at the seemingly unconscious man. "Can you hear me, Bum?" He scrambled for his phone. Dialed 911. *Lord, please let him be okay.*

Sadie rushed into the room, screeching to a halt when she spotted Bum on the floor.

"Uncle Mickey?" Her lip quivered.

"It's okay, princess. Mr. Bum just fell, but I need to get him some help." It had taken all of his effort to keep his voice calm. Just then, the dispatcher came on the line. Mick relayed the information as succinctly as he could, adding that he suspected his friend was having a heart attack.

Ending the call, he looked at Sadie who was sitting in a chair, her eyes wide. "Mr. Bum isn't feeling well, so the people from the hospital are on their way to help him."

Bum started to rouse. "What happened?" He looked around. "What am I—?" He tried to sit up, but Mick stopped him.

"Easy, my friend. Ambulance is on its way."

"Ambulance?" Bum frowned.

"I think that heartburn might be indicating a problem with your heart. We need to get you checked out." To Mick's surprise, the man didn't argue. It was as if he'd had the same suspicions. "Have you got some aspirin? They told me I should give you one."

The man nodded and pointed toward the collection of bottles beside the sink.

Sassy wiggled toward them as Mick stood, her ears back, tail low as she sniffed her master.

Mick was certain the dog sensed something was wrong. Especially when she plopped down beside the big man and nosed at his hand.

"It's okay, Sassy." Bum stroked the animal.

Mick located the aspirin and filled a glass with water. Looking down at his friend, Mick knew he couldn't let him go to the hospital alone. Bum's daughters lived in Dallas and Abilene, and while Mick would let them know what was going on, they were a minimum of four hours away. Still, he hated to make Sadie go with him.

"Sadie, I'm going to see if you can stay with Miss Christa while I go to the hospital with Mr. Bum, okay?" He hated to do it, but she was his only option.

"Okay. But can Sassy come, too? Cuz we

can't leave her here all alone. And I know Dixie will love her."

"We'll see what Miss Christa says." He dialed her number and waited while it rang. Just when he was about to give up, she answered.

"Mick? Hey, I'm still over here at Laurel's."

"I'm sorry to interrupt, but I need your help. Bum collapsed and I'm waiting for an ambulance. I think it's his heart."

"Where are you?"

"At Bum's."

"I'm on my way."

He could hear the ambulance approaching as the line went dead. *God, please don't take Bum away from me now. I'm not sure I could bear losing another loved one so soon.*

When the EMTs arrived, Mick explained what happened and answered questions before taking Sadie outside to wait for Christa. He glanced up at the brilliant blue sky, wondering how such a beautiful day could turn ugly so fast.

The sound of tires moving over gravel had him shifting his attention to the drive and Christa's SUV.

Once she parked, Sadie hurried to meet her.

Mick joined them a moment later.

"How is he?" Christa rested her hands atop Sadie's shoulders.

"Probably won't know much until they get him to the hospital."

"I was praying all the way here. I told Wes and Laurel. They're praying, too, and they activated the church's prayer chain."

Hands on his hips, Mick couldn't help but chuckle. "Well, I reckon everyone in town ought to know by the time we get to the hospital then." A sound had him turning to see the EMTs wheeling Bum out on a gurney. Mick moved toward them.

An oxygen mask covered his friend's nose and mouth, but his color was still ashen.

Mick reached for the man's hand. "You know, if you were trying to get out of doing the dishes, you could have just asked."

Bum managed a weak smile.

Mick eyed one of the EMTs. "I'll follow you to the hospital."

While they loaded Bum into the ambulance, Mick rejoined Christa and Sadie. "I don't know how long I'll be."

Christa held up a hand. "Doesn't matter. Sadie is fine with me. You just take care of Bum."

"Can we take Sassy?" Sadie eyed a confused Christa.

"Bum's shih tzu," Mick added.

"Sure. Dixie would love having another play-mate." She hugged Sadie.

Mick caught Christa's attention, hating that he still hadn't been able to tell her about the Gebhardt building. "I'm sorry I interrupted your time with Laurel." He shrugged. "I didn't know who else to call."

"Mick, there's no need to apologize. You look after Bum, and we'll see you when you get back."

Mick spent the following hours contacting Bum's daughters, Sandy and Carrie, and field-ing incoming calls from well-meaning church members and townsfolk asking what they could do. He told them all to pray, knowing that was all they could do right now and what Bum needed most.

When the doctor informed Mick they were transferring Bum to a hospital in Houston, Mick notified the man's daughters of the change, en-couraging them to go straight there. Then Mick waited with his friend, praying with him before he was loaded into another ambulance.

Piling into his truck at almost seven thirty, Mick felt completely drained. Emotionally, physically. And he still had to talk with Christa.

He knocked on her door a short time later, feeling as weary as he would if he'd been working fence all day. Instead, he'd done nothing but sit around, worrying and praying.

Christa opened the door, looking like a breath of fresh air. "How is he?"

Mick relayed everything as he followed her into the kitchen.

"You look exhausted. Can I get you something to eat?"

"No, I'm good." Except he wasn't good. He still had to come clean with her. But if he thought his mind had been muddled last night—"Where's Sadie?"

"On the couch, watching—"

"Let me guess. *Frozen.*"

"Of course."

He moved to the opening between the kitchen and dining room to check on his niece. She was sitting on the sofa with a snoozing Sassy at her side. Yet while Sadie sat upright, her head kept bobbing, and she was barely able to keep her eyes open.

"I think she's ready for bed," Christa whispered over his shoulder.

"Yeah." He faced her now, longing to take her into his arms. "Sassy, too."

"I know you wanted to talk about something, but I can tell you're spent." She rubbed his upper arm, her warmth seeping into him. "Why don't we wait until tomorrow?"

Waiting would only prolong the agony. But right now he wasn't sure he could string the words together in a way that wouldn't be misunderstood. "Tomorrow it is, then."

After the early-morning rush on Monday, Christa worked alongside Patsy on the store's spring window display. They'd started with some faux grass, added a bench and a small wheelbarrow. Now it was time to add all those little things people would need for springtime planting. Shovels and spades, watering cans, gardening gloves, colorful pots and a multitude of other things.

Christa positioned an old soda crate atop a small outdoor table. "Patsy, what do you know about the Gebhardt building?"

"You mean the one next door?" The woman pointed, as if there was more than one Gebhardt building in Bliss.

"Yes."

Patsy filled a bright green metal bucket with a selection of seed packets. "Used to be one of them old mercantile places. You know, a general store. I went in there once or twice when I was real little. About all I remember, though, are the wooden shelves and the jars of penny candy on the counter by the old cash register."

"Sounds like a cool place." Christa took the

now-full bucket from Patsy and set it atop the crate. Just the pop of color she wanted.

"Yeah, there's been a lot of stuff in there since it closed in the midseventies, but nothing near as interesting."

Straightening, Christa stretched her back. "Why'd it close?"

Patsy shrugged. "Louise Ashford's parents had taken it over when her grandparents retired, but Louise had no interest in running the place, so when her folks retired they just put it up for rent."

"Ashford?" A sick feeling began to stir in Christa's gut.

"Louise was Mick's mama."

Christa's gaze narrowed. "Who owns the building now?"

"I reckon Mick and his sister." Patsy adjusted her ponytail. "Well, make that Mick, now that Jen is gone." She shook her head. "So sad."

The sick feeling Christa had threatened to turn into a full revolt. Mick owned the Gebhardt building, yet he never said a word the other night when she'd gone on and on about her desire for the space. Instead, Mick had lied to her, just like Brody. She didn't care if it was a lie by omission. A lie was still a lie.

Anger propelled her from the window into the

store. "Patsy, would you mind finishing this up for me? I have someplace I have to be."

Without waiting for her assistant manager to respond, she retrieved her purse from her office and went outside to her SUV. She would not let Mick get away with this.

Gray clouds raced across the sky as she drove toward the ranch. Just like Brody, Mick had been using her. He didn't care about her feelings or her dreams. He only wanted someone to help him with Sadie. And she'd allowed herself to be played. Again. How foolish could she be?

As she pulled into the main drive, Mick's truck was coming out. Ignoring him, she continued into her driveway and got out, hoping he would follow.

He did.

The wind whipped her hair into her face as she crossed her arms over her chest and waited.

Finally, he pulled alongside her, smiling as he stepped out and moved toward her. "Hey, I was just on my way to see you." Hands dangling from the pockets of his faded jeans, he stopped in front of her.

"How could you?" She shoved a hand against his chest. "You lied to me." Tears threatened but she willed them away, refusing to give him the satisfaction.

Rubbing his chest as though she'd hurt him, he said, "Huh?"

"I *know* that you own the Gebhardt building."

He heaved a sigh, appearing suddenly crest-fallen. "That's what I've been wanting to tell you."

"Oh, sure. Now that you've been outed." Scraping her hair behind her ears, she glared at him. "Yet you let me sit beside that fire and pour my heart out to you without ever saying a word. You even encouraged me to rent." And she'd actually been pondering some of his recommendations! "Who does that?"

"Christa, I'm sorry. I promise you, I never meant to deceive or hurt you in any way. I was confused. I'd made the decision to hold on to the building for Sadie, but when you said—"

"Save it." She threw up a hand as the breeze whipped between them. "I don't want to hear your excuses."

"*Please*. I was confused, all right?"

"Oh, and you couldn't have told me that?" Fists balled at her sides, she continued. "I would have understood. Instead, you allowed me to keep talking like some fool."

"No." He took a step closer, gravel crunching beneath his boots. "I'd never think of you as a fool, Christa. You're the smartest person I've ever known."

"Yeah, well, right about now, I'm feeling pretty stupid for allowing you into my life." Not to mention her heart. Twice, she'd fallen in love. And twice, she'd been duped. "You didn't trust me with the truth, Mick."

Hands slung low on his hips, he hung his head. "You're right. I'm sorry." He looked her in the eye. "I should have told you right from the start."

"But you didn't. So how can I ever trust you again?"

"Aw, come on, Christa. You know that's not true. Of course you can trust me."

She shook her head. "No, I can't." Turning, she started toward the house, her heart feeling as though it had been turned inside out.

"I love you, Christa."

Her steps halted, her eyes closing. How long had she wanted to hear those words from him? Now they meant nothing.

"I know you think I'm just saying that, but I mean it. I've never cared about any woman the way I care for you."

Thanks to the gravel, she could hear him drawing closer, yet she couldn't seem to make her feet move. So she stared at the sky.

"From the moment I wake up until the time I fall asleep, you're on my mind. You consume me in a way I've never experienced before. It's as frightening as it is exciting." He was right behind her now. "I love you. And I know you're mad, but I think you might love me, too."

With a deep breath, she turned to face him. "Love and trust go hand in hand, Mick. You can't have one without the other. You betrayed my trust by withholding the truth." This time, she ran toward the house, unable to risk being stopped again. Because if he told her he loved her one more time, she just might believe him.

Chapter Fifteen

Mick pulled up to Bum's house just after one on Thursday afternoon, feeling like his insides had tangled with a shredder. He'd been miserable ever since Christa came at him Monday. Throw in the fact that he was due in court a week from today, and he wasn't sure he could feel much worse.

Hard to believe it was only a few days ago that Mick sat in Bum's kitchen, telling God that he couldn't bear to lose someone else he loved. Yet that's exactly what had happened. Only it had been Christa who Mick had lost. All because he hadn't been man enough to tell her the truth.

He opened the door of his truck, eager to see how his friend was feeling. And perhaps get some fatherly advice. A wiggly Sassy flew across his lap.

"Guess you're ready to be back home, huh, Sassy." Sadie sure was going to miss having a dog in the house. He had a feeling she'd wear him down at some point, and they'd end up with a furry friend of their own.

After retrieving the two sudoku puzzle books he'd picked up at the store, he climbed out and closed the door. Bum loved his sudokus, and with him having to take things easy for a while, Mick figured they'd be a good way for him to pass the time.

Sassy waited at his feet, whining, as he knocked on the door. "Hang in there, Sass. We're almost there."

A moment later, Sandy swung it wide and the dog bounded inside.

"Sassy, girl. You're home." She stooped to pet the fur ball. "Go get Daddy."

The dog took off as Sandy stood. "Thank you for keeping her, Mick." She motioned for him to come in, then greeted him with a hug. He and the woman with long blond hair had practically grown up together. Their fathers were best friends and she'd been a year ahead of Mick in high school, while her sister had been two years behind him.

"Where's Carrie?"

"She had to head on back to Dallas yesterday." She closed the door. "Dad's been hoping you'd stop by."

"Oh, yeah?"

She nodded. "Right now, I'm pretty sure he thinks of me as the enemy."

"Now why would that be?"

"Because I'm the one telling him what to do, making sure he eats right and all that other stuff he hates."

"I ain't deaf you know." Bum's voice came from around the corner in the living room. "I can hear everything y'all are saying."

Mick couldn't help laughing. "Sounds like he's back to normal."

"He's gettin' there." She led Mick into the living room where Bum sat in his leather recliner, wearing a scowl. "I have some laundry to tend to, so I'll leave the two of you alone."

"'Bout time," Bum sputtered. Petting the dog who was now in his lap, he continued. "She's been hoverin' ever since she and her sister got to the hospital. Now that the nurses aren't around, Miss High-and-Mighty thinks she's in charge."

Mick eased onto the leather sofa. "Nah, she just wants to see you up and about again. Like the rest of us."

"I ain't made for all this sittin'."

"Sassy doesn't seem to mind." Mick nodded toward the dog.

"Of course she doesn't. She'd sit here all day if I'd let her." He scrubbed the dog's neck. "Me? I got things to do."

"Oh, settle down, Bum. It's only for a little while. I've got your cattle covered."

The man glowered. "Whose side are you on anyway?"

"And here I thought you went to the hospital, but judging by the way you're acting, it must have been elementary school."

His friend harrumphed. "Aren't you the funny one?"

"Here." Mick stood long enough to hand the man the puzzle books. "Maybe these will keep you busy."

Sassy hopped down as Bum grabbed his readers from the side table to peer at the books. "Yeah, they might help for a little while. Thanks." Removing the glasses, he looked at Mick. "Did you ever talk with Christa?"

Resting one ankle on the opposite knee, Mick swiped at the dust on his boot. "Oh, I talked to her all right. Though she did most of the talking."

"And?" Bum sounded so hopeful.

Meanwhile, Mick didn't have a shred of hope left. "She hates me, Bum."

The older man leaned closer. "She said that?"

"No, I inferred it. Somehow she found out

that I owned the building before I got the chance to tell her. She called me a liar and said she could never trust me again."

"Did you explain why you hadn't said anything?"

"I tried, but she wasn't willing to listen." He glanced down at the carpet where Sassy was chewing on one of her toys. "I hurt her, Bum. Hurt her real bad. And I miss her something fierce."

"I'm sorry, son. I know you really cared about her."

"I still do."

"Yeah, love ain't somethin' you can just turn off, is it?"

Mick cut a look in his friend's direction. "Did I tell you I was in love with Christa?"

Smiling, Bum said, "You didn't have to, Mick. It's written all over your face whenever you so much as think about her."

"So how come Christa didn't see that?"

"I expect she did." The man paused for a moment, his hands splayed over the arms of the recliner. "How's Sadie taking it? She and Christa spent a lot of time together."

"She misses her. But how do you explain to a five-year-old that the person they love doesn't want to be there because of your stupidity?"

"Maybe Christa will come around after a

while. After the hurt dissipates and she can think about what you said with a clear head."

Nervous energy had Mick standing. "That'd be great, but I'm not going to hold my breath." He moved to the window beside the fireplace and eyed the lone longhorn grazing among the Black Angus in the pasture.

"Don't tell me you're just going to give up?" Bum's voice held a hint of disbelief.

Turning to face him, Mick said, "What else am I supposed to do? She doesn't want to see or talk to me."

"Well, God's word says that love is patient."

"You ought to know better than anyone that patience isn't my strong suit."

Bum looked at him through his shaggy eyebrows. "Mick, you've waited forty-five years to find love. Surely you're not going to just let it go without a fight."

The man had a good point. "But how do I fight? What should I do?"

"Just keep on loving her however you feel led. She may have given up on love, so it's up to you to show her that it's worth a second chance."

Was Bum right? Could Mick really win back Christa's heart?

Maybe not. But just because she stopped caring for him didn't mean he had to stop caring for her. And he cared, all right. More than he realized.

He thought about the hearing next week. Christa was supposed to testify on his behalf, and he was pretty sure she'd still do that. But going in there without her by his side? That was going to be tough.

I will never leave thee, nor forsake thee. The words played across Mick's heart, reminding him there was one person he could count on. The One who'd been with him since he prayed that prayer in vacation Bible school when he was ten years old. God was his strength and his defender. His help in times of trouble.

Mick needed to cling to that now more than ever. And trust that if Christa was the woman for him, then God would work things out.

Christa brushed the snickerdoodle crumbs from her shirt as she stepped out of her SUV in front of Bum's house after work Friday. She still hadn't figured out who'd left the trio of cookies and a caramel macchiato on her desk this afternoon, but they'd been a bright spot in an otherwise dreary day.

Armed with a loaf of low-fat banana bread, she glanced up at the gray clouds that had brought them rain for much of the day, her heart heavy. She missed Mick. And Sadie. What she wouldn't give for one of Sadie's hugs right about now. Still, she knew she had to learn to move forward without them, because she wasn't willing to risk her heart to someone who would lie to her.

She strode onto the covered porch, knocked on the six-panel double door and waited.

A few seconds later, a trim blonde who appeared close to her own age opened the door, Sassy wiggling at her feet. "Can I help you?" Blue eyes that looked a lot like Bum's held a smile.

"Hi, I'm Christa Slocum." She stooped to pet the dog who was now circling her feet. "I live just up the road and go to church with Bum." She stood. "Is he receiving visitors?"

"He sure is." She motioned for Christa to enter. "Matter of fact, he's going a little stir-crazy, so guests are his connection to the outside world."

"I can imagine him struggling with being cooped up."

"Honey, you don't know the half of it." They both laughed. "I'm Sandy, by the way. Bum's daughter."

"It's nice to meet you."

Sandy led her into a room with a vaulted ceiling, leather furniture and a limestone fireplace with a huge brown-and-white longhorn head mounted over the mantel. "You have company, Dad."

Bum looked up with a quick smile as Sassy jumped into his lap. "Christa, aren't you a sight for sore eyes."

She approached his recliner and gave him a brief hug. "You're looking much better than the last time I saw you."

"Yeah, well."

"I brought you some homemade banana bread." She glanced at Sandy. "It's low-fat."

"Now why'd you have to go and ruin it by sayin' that?" Bum scowled.

"I was skeptical, too," said Christa, "but I think you'll be pleasantly surprised."

"I'll leave you two to chat," said Sandy.

"You don't have to leave." Christa hated to think she'd chased her off.

"That's all right. I need to call home and check in with my kids."

"Have a seat." Bum gestured toward the couch. "How are you doing?"

She perched on the edge of the cushion. "I think I'm supposed to be asking you that."

"Ah, I'm right as rain." He shifted in his seat to make more room for Sassy. "Least once they let me get back to work." His friendly blue eyes seemed to bore into her. "Mick told me what happened."

She drew in a deep breath and simply nodded.

"I know you feel like Mick lied to you and that it stings like crazy, but he never set out to hurt you, Christa. That boy's got a heart of gold."

"I know he does."

"What you may not know is that he doesn't open that heart to too many people. You were blessed to be one of them. Problem is, he didn't just open his heart to you, he plum gave it away."

Her cheeks warmed and she offered a nervous smile. Bum was the last person she'd expected to have this kind of conversation with. Then again, he did think of Mick as a son. But it made her uncomfortable.

"Yeah, Mick messed up," he continued. "We country boys are prone to that sometimes." He smiled. "But when we love, we give it everything we've got."

While she appreciated his insight, she needed to get out of there. "I'll be honest, Bum, there's a part of me that really wants to believe that. But the bigger part of me, the one that's been jaded by the lies of someone else I thought loved me, is afraid to take that risk again." She shrugged. "Once bitten, twice shy. Except I've been bitten twice."

"Don't judge Mick on the actions of someone else. That's not fair to him or you."

She thought for a moment. "I suppose you're right." She stood. "And I'll try to keep that in mind. I need to get home to my Dixie, though. She's probably crossing her legs."

"All right, young lady. You take care of yourself."

Driving a mile up the road to her farmhouse, she couldn't help thinking about what Bum said. It was wrong to judge Mick based on Brody's actions. They were two completely different people, and Mick was a far better man than Brody ever thought about being. But the fact that Mick had evaded the truth, dancing his way around it by suggesting she have a cute little storefront, still irked her. If he'd have simply come clean, they wouldn't be where they were now. But he hadn't.

She pulled into the main drive, bumping over the cattle guard, and again when she turned into her drive. *God, when will my heart stop hurting?*

Gathering her purse, she stepped out of the vehicle.

"Miss Christa."

Stunned, she jerked her head up to see Sadie running toward her from the porch. "Sadie?" She embraced the child, whose arms went around Christa's hips. "What are you doing here?"

The girl took a step back and looked up at her. "I misseded you."

She couldn't help but smile. "I've missed you, too." She scanned the yard and the porch looking for Mick. "Where's your uncle?"

"At the camp house."

Alarm bells went off in Christa's head. "Does he know you're here?"

Just then her phone buzzed. She tugged it from the back pocket of her jeans to see Mick's name on the screen. Looked like she had her answer.

Sending Sadie a look of disapproval, she answered the call. "Hello."

"I can't find Sadie." Panic filled his voice. "If you see her, please—"

"She's here with me. I just got home to find her waiting."

"Oh, thank God." His relief crackled through the line. "I'll be right there."

Ending the call, she eyed the child before her. "All right, Sadie, would you care to tell me what's going on?"

"I wanted to see you." Her bottom lip pooched out.

"Then why didn't you ask your Uncle Mickey to contact me?"

"I did. He said you didn't want to talk to him."

Christa heaved a sigh, wondering if this was

what divorce was like when kids were involved. "Come on. I need to let Dixie out." She knew seeing Mick was inevitable. They were neighbors, after all. Still, while her mind continually replayed all the reasons why she should not be with him, she wasn't sure how her heart would react to seeing him. She'd better get used to it, though.

Sadie was chasing Dixie around the yard when Mick's truck pulled into her drive. She could see his anxiety the moment he stepped out of his vehicle. A mixture of anger, relief and sheer terror pinched his handsome features as he strode toward Sadie.

"Sadie Louise Sanderson, what are you doing up here?"

His niece pouted. "I wanted to see Miss Christa and you wouldn't let me talk to her."

He glanced Christa's way. "I didn't say I wouldn't. I know you and Miss Christa have a very special relationship."

One that had fallen victim to her dismissal of Mick. Christa should have been more sensitive. Instead of focusing on her feelings, she should have thought about how her and Mick's breakup—as if they were ever a couple—would impact the precious little girl who was still coming to terms with the loss of her parents.

"How did you get up here, anyway?" He stared at his niece.

"I walkeded. But I weared my rubber boots." She lifted her foot to show him.

"At least the only traffic around here is you and me." Christa forced herself to meet Mick's gaze. "Sadie, why don't you play with Dixie while your Uncle Mickey and I talk."

"Okay. Come on, Dixie." They took off across the yard.

Mick lifted his hat and thrust his hand through his hair. "She scared the fire out of me. I was only puttin' laundry away, and when I came downstairs, she was nowhere to be found. I was afraid she'd fallen into the cow pond or something."

"I was pretty surprised to see her here. I would have called once I'd finished grilling her, but you beat me to it."

He met her gaze, and she wished she could smooth away those lines that creased his forehead. "She loves you, you know?"

"And I love her, too. I'd be happy to have her visit or spend the night. And she can always call and talk to me."

He nodded. "I appreciate that."

"Have you told her yet? About the custody hearing?"

"No." He watched Sadie play. "I'm afraid of how she'll react. But I will. Soon."

"If I can help in any way, just let me know."

His attention returned to Christa. "Are you doing all right?"

"Yeah, I'm just fine." The words tumbled out too quickly. But seeing Mick, the depth of his concern and love for Sadie, only reminded her of what she was missing.

"Good. Don't hesitate to let me know if you need anything."

She nodded, then stood there in awkward silence. No more teasing jabs like they'd exchanged even before Sadie came to live with him, no laughter. They were barely friends.

"Let me grab Sadie, and we'll be out of your way."

After hugging Sadie goodbye, Christa watched as they climbed into Mick's truck and drove away, wondering if this was how it was always going to be. Because if it was, she wasn't sure she could bear it.

Her phone rang and when she looked at the screen, she saw Jade's name. "Hello."

"Oh, good. I was afraid you wouldn't answer."

"What is it, Jade?"

"The company I told you about seems to have their heart set on you. I told them you weren't interested, but they insisted I try one more time. Something about third time being a charm."

As Mick's truck disappeared into the woods, grief wove its way through Christa. Perhaps the timing of this call was God's way of telling her it was time to move on. At least in corporate life she'd have plenty of work to bury herself under and she'd never have to feel.

"Tell you what, Jade. I will speak with them, but only by phone or video chat. If they won't consent to that, then I have no interest."

"All right. I'll let you know what they say."

Returning the phone to her back pocket, she looked from Dixie to the farmhouse she'd painstakingly restored, fulfilling a long-time dream.

Her gaze shifted to the winding road that led to Mick's camp house. For the briefest of moments, a new dream had ignited. One she'd never imagined. But that dream had been extinguished by a lie. Perhaps it was never meant to be. Yet she wasn't sure she could live with the daily reminders of what might have been.

Chapter Sixteen

For whatever reason, Bliss Hardware was particularly busy on Friday. Perhaps the spring window display coupled with warmer than usual weather and the promise of a gorgeous weekend had folks eager to shake off their winter blues and move headlong into summer. Christa was not about to complain, though. She just wished she hadn't scheduled her video interview for this afternoon. She hadn't stopped all day. Fortunately, her friend Rae had sent over lunch from her café. Someone must have told her how busy things were. It was nice to have somebody anticipate her needs.

Now the sun beat down on her SUV as she made her way home. Trying to stay focused on her interview would be nearly impossible at the store. Way too many distractions and potential interruptions. And after looking over the information Jade had emailed, Christa had determined to give it her full attention. Yes, it would mean leaving Bliss, a place she loved and had come to think of as home, but could she remain here, seeing Mick day after day, sharing fleeting moments with Sadie, always wondering what might have been?

As she approached the drive, she saw Mick on his big tractor and her heart skipped a beat. What was he doing there? And why was he blocking her driveway?

Drawing closer, she noticed that her cattle guard had been removed and he was cleaning out the ditch beneath it that had collected all sorts of dirt and debris.

Hmm… Just like he'd said he would that day she offered to help him with Sadie's room.

Something about that made her smile, and not only because it meant her flowers and fountain grass would be safe from that brown cow and her wandering ways. Mick was a man of his word. Someone who followed through. Traits she admired. But lying? Not so much.

She parked far enough away to where her vehicle wouldn't be in his way, then tried to figure out how to get in. It was either leap over the chasm where the cattle guard had once been— which would be nearly impossible given she was not an expert hurdler—or shimmy between the barbed wires on the fence, which she'd seen Mick do plenty of times.

The warm midafternoon sun beat down on her as she moved toward the fence. She slipped one leg between the horizontal wires, bending at the waist to slide her torso through. Simple enough. Until her Bliss Hardware shirt got caught on one of the barbs. She tried to break free, but she only managed to make things worse.

Chagrin heated her cheeks when she saw Mick coming toward her.

"You look like you could use a little help." He stepped on the lower wire, his boot drawing it to the ground, then freed her shirt, allowing her to pass through.

"Thank you." Standing on the opposite side of the fence, she couldn't help noticing his muscular arms, how his biceps tested the sleeves of his gray T-shirt.

"What are you doing home this time of day?"

"I've got a video call at two and the store has too many distractions."

"Must be important."

Considering it could determine whether or not she stayed in Bliss… "Yeah." But did she dare tell him she was thinking about leaving? How would he feel about that? And why did she care?

"I, uh—" she pointed toward the house "—I need to run." She glanced toward the cattle guard. "Thank you for addressing this."

He lifted a shoulder. "I told you I would." He touched the brim of his hat then and gave her a nod—something that never failed to set her heart to fluttering.

But she didn't have time for fluttering of any kind. She hurried toward the house, well aware that she needed to look and behave in a professional manner for this call. So, after letting Dixie outside, she swapped her polo shirt for a blouse, then touched up her makeup and added a hint of color to her lips.

She let Dixie back inside before making her way to the upstairs bedroom that she used as an office, the one that overlooked the driveway. It was a good thing her desk was on the opposite side of the room so she wouldn't be staring at Mick the whole time.

She'd barely settled into her chair when the call came through. With a deep breath, she answered it on her tablet.

"Christa, it's good to see you again."

Her body tensed. Was this some sort of joke? What was Brody doing on the other side of the screen? He'd let his dark hair grow out and had it slicked back. And he was wearing the red power tie she'd given him for his birthday back when she'd been sucked in by his charm. She knew better now.

"So you're the client who's had Jade pestering me?"

"You're the only person I know who enjoys a challenge as much as I do, and I've got an opportunity that's not only perfect for you, it's one you're probably going to thank me for."

As if she'd want to thank him for anything. "What makes you say that?"

"Oh, come on, Christa. You and I were like two peas in a pod. We're both driven to be the best and make the most money doing it."

She may be driven, but they were definitely *not* the same. Unlike Brody, Christa cared about other people and liked helping them make *their* lives better, not just her own.

"Let's cut to the chase. Tell me about the company and the position."

"Drago Web Services offers cloud services that allow companies of any size to run almost everything in the cloud. And our growth— particularly in the area of start-ups—has been faster than projected. I would like to bring you on board as a start-up account manager to help propel the growth of high-potential early, mid- and late-stage start-ups."

While Christa may not have any interest in Brody, the opportunity he presented thoroughly intrigued her. This was the type of position she'd once dreamed of. Helping start-up businesses build and thrive. It was a challenge she could sink her teeth into and prove to herself what she was capable of.

For the better part of the next hour, she listened, voiced her concerns and asked questions. Starting with location.

"You'd be right here in Austin. Our old stomping grounds." He paused a moment. "I've missed you, Christa. We always did make a good team, and if we were to pair up on this, the sky's the limit. We'd have everything we always wanted."

We? As she recalled, his *we* had really been more of a *me*. Brody only thought of himself.

And looking at him now, she couldn't believe she'd actually been interested in him, let alone wanted a future with him. He was still a self-absorbed jerk who'd sell his own mother if he thought it would benefit him. Unlike Mick, who was doing his best to right a little girl's world that had been turned upside down.

When it came to business, though, Brody had a keen eye for picking winners. And based on what she'd just learned about this company, she couldn't argue.

"Brody, this sounds like a promising opportunity. But I'm going to need some time to think and pray on it. I've been away from that world for almost five years."

"And I have no doubt you'd snap right back."

That's what she was afraid of. But was that what she wanted to do? Was it what God wanted her to do?

"I'll get back to you soon." Ending the call, she stood, rubbing her arms as she rounded the desk. She couldn't believe she was considering this. She'd always been content in Bliss. She loved her store, her farmhouse, the people.

Approaching the window, she saw that Mick had finished. The cattle guard was back in place, and his tractor was gone.

I know you feel like Mick lied to you and that it stings like crazy, but he never set out to hurt you, Christa. Bum's words replayed in her mind. *He didn't just open his heart to you, he plum gave it away.*

She squeezed her eyes shut, wishing she could believe that. Her time with Mick and Sadie had filled parts of her she wasn't even aware were there, and for a brief moment, she'd felt loved.

But those times were over. Her idyllic life had evaporated.

Peering out the window again, she found herself faced with a choice. Stay and live with the constant reminders of what she'd lost, or return to her former life and lose herself in her work.

* * *

Mick stared out the open window of his truck as he waited in the line of vehicles slowly inching their way toward the elementary school for student pick-up Friday afternoon. A warm breeze sifted through an ancient live oak on the playground, sending its spent leaves drifting aimlessly toward the ground as new buds pushed forth.

Watching Christa walk away earlier today had him realizing that he'd lost everyone he'd ever loved. His parents, Jen and Kyle, Christa. All he had left was Sadie, and if he lost her—

No! He could not think that way. Sadie deserved to be in a home where she was loved and wanted. Not treated as a possession the Sandersons paid no mind to unless it was convenient for them. He had to fight to make sure Jen and Kyle's wishes were upheld.

Taking his foot off the brake, he kept an eye on the sedan in front of him as he rolled forward. The hearing was less than a week away, and he had yet to mention anything to Sadie. He sure wished Christa could be there to help him. To fill in the blanks or smooth things over when he said something that wasn't quite right.

He scrubbed a hand over his face. Man, he missed her. They'd made a good team, though she was definitely the better half.

Some country breakup song started on the radio, and he promptly turned it off. He didn't need to feel lower than he already did. Seeing Christa today had been as tough as it was unexpected. If she hadn't gotten caught on that fence, he would have stayed on his tractor where he couldn't see the hurt in her pretty hazel eyes or be tormented by her apple-scented shampoo. Instead, he was left longing to hold her, trying to play it cool and pretend he was fine with being only friends.

What was she doing there in the middle of the day anyway? Something about a video call. If it pertained to store business, wouldn't she have wanted to do that at the store, regardless of distractions?

Lord, I miss her so much. I never meant to hurt Christa. God, I'd give just about anything to have another chance with her, but that may not be a part of Your plan. If that's the case, then help me to accept it. But if it's not, if Christa is the one for me, show me what to do.

Once he had Sadie, the two of them made their weekly run to the grocery store. And just like every other time, when they were finished, the amount of items in their bags far exceeded what had been on his list. One of these days he'd have to stop being such a pushover where his niece was concerned.

When they arrived back at the ranch, he heard Sadie sigh behind him as they passed Christa's place.

"I bet Dixie misses me."

He eyed her in the rearview mirror as he veered off toward the camp house. "I'm sure she does, princess."

After hauling the groceries inside, he stood at the island to unload them.

Perched atop the opposite side of the counter, Sadie munched on her fruit snacks. "How come Miss Christa doesn't come over anymore?"

His chest tightened. "We talked about this, Sadie. Miss Christa and I had an argument."

She ignored her treat long enough to send him a look that said she was on to him. "You fighted."

Taking a bunch of bananas from a bag, he chuckled. "Yeah, sort of." He set them by the window over the sink.

"How come?"

Finding a way to explain adult things to a five-year-old was always a challenge for him, but he was getting better. "Well, there was something I should have done that I didn't. And when she found out, it made her very sad. She felt like she couldn't trust me anymore."

Sadie tilted her little head, looking at him as though she was truly trying to wrap her brain around this conversation. Then again, she probably was, because she really missed Christa. "Why don't you just tell her you're sorry?"

"I did." Putting the eggs and bacon in the refrigerator, he continued. "But she was pretty angry with me. So she doesn't want to be around me much anymore. However—" closing the door, he returned to the island and met her gaze, wanting her to understand "—she still loves you just as much as she did before."

Without missing a beat, she asked, "Does she love you?"

He wished. "I don't think so, Sadie."

She wadded up the empty wrapper and handed it to him. "Do you love her?"

Did the kid know how to go for the jugular or what? "Yeah, I do. A lot."

She fell silent as he moved the canned goods and numerous boxes of mac and cheese to the cupboard. Finally, "Uncle Mickey?"

"Yeah?" He watched her as he gathered up the empty grocery bags.

"Do you want to marry Miss Christa?"

Oh, to live in a world where life was so simple. "Well, I never thought about—wait, that's not true. I have thought about it a time or two."

"So… *Do* you want to marry her?"

He had to laugh. "Yes, all right. I want to marry Miss Christa."

"Good, cuz I want you to marry her, too."

He lifted her off the counter and set her feet on the floor he still hoped to replace. "Oh, you do, huh?"

"Yes." She gave one firm nod. "You *hafta* ask her."

He stared down at her. "Princess, it's not that simple."

"Yes, it is. You getted a ring, you tell her you love her *so much*—" she threw her arms wide "—then she says yes, and you live happily-eber-after." She sighed, holding her hands against her chest. "It's like a dream come true."

Shaking his head, he said, "Now where did you hear that?"

She frowned up at him. "*Everybody* says it, Uncle Mickey."

"Oh, they do, huh?" A dream come true. He froze. "Sadie, I think you might be on to something."

"What?"

"A dream come true."

Her hand went to her hip. "That's what I said."

He lifted her into his arms. "Sadie, I don't know if Miss Christa will marry me or not, but I think I can make her dream come true."

"Really?"

"Really."

"Okay." She nodded. "Let's do it."

Chapter Seventeen

"You're leaving us?" Laurel's eyes were wide, as were Rae's and Paisley's as they stared at Christa across her desk at Bliss Hardware Saturday afternoon.

Leaning back in her office chair, she gulped. "Come on, guys. I've been offered an amazing opportunity."

"I thought you hated corporate life." Rae crossed her arms over her chest, her blue eyes boring into Christa.

"This will give me a chance to help others build their businesses."

"Yeah, so they can become cutthroat jerks." Her favorite barista huffed.

"What about Mick and Sadie?" Paisley tilted her head, sending her long red braid spilling over her shoulder.

"They have their own life." One she'd give anything to be a part of.

Her three best friends looked at each other.

"What happened?" Laurel's tone held a note of sympathy.

After a moment, she gave in to their pleading looks and told them about her desire to expand the store and everything that had transpired in the last week.

Rae shifted in her seat. "I guess that explains the special deliveries Mick asked for."

Christa looked at her. "What deliveries?"

"The macchiato and cookies. Lunch yesterday."

"That was Mick?" Christa wasn't sure how to feel about that.

"Yes, he said he knew you were too busy to stop, so he wanted to help you out." Her brow lifted. "I just assumed you knew."

"No."

"So you've decided to run away."

Christa shifted her attention to Paisley, who sat there stone-faced, arms crossed tightly over her chest, one leg over the other, bobbing it at a frenzied pace. "No." She thought about seeing Mick yesterday and how much it hurt knowing she couldn't be with him. "He should have told me as soon as I revealed I was the one wanting to buy the Gebhardt building. But he didn't say a word until I confronted him with the truth." Resting her elbow on her desk, she plunked her chin in her hand. "Why is it that every guy I like feels the need to lie to me?"

Uncrossing her legs, Paisley leaned forward. "Mick isn't Brody, Christa." Gripping the edges of her chair, she added, "Before you had this little exchange with Mick, how did you feel about him?"

Christa lifted a shoulder, refusing to look at her friends. "At first I thought my feelings were just about Sadie. But the more we were together, the more I realized he was a tender-hearted man who was willing to do almost anything for someone he loved. Just the kind of man I'd always dreamed of finding. Until he *lied*."

Laurel stood and moved around the desk to grab a piece of chocolate from Christa's emergency stash. "I don't think Mick's hesitance can compare with what Brody did. Brody was calculated and self-serving. Mick is grieving his sister and learning to be a father." She set a hand on Christa's shoulder. "He deserves a little grace."

Paisley cleared her throat. "I think the real problem here, Christa, is you."

"What? Why?" She shoved her chair back and grabbed the entire bucket of candy.

"I think you're afraid."

"Of Mick?" She fished out a Tootsie Roll before setting her stash on the desk.

"Of love. Or more to the point, of *losing* someone you love." Paisley cocked her head. "It's easier to send him away on your terms than to risk your heart again."

Tears sprang to Christa's eyes. Her friend knew her too well. "How can you say that when you lost your husband and child?"

"Better to have loved and lost than to never have loved at all, my friend." Standing, Paisley moved toward Christa. "I miss Peter and Logan terribly. But I was so blessed to have had them in my life if only for a little while." She paused a moment to ward off her emotions. "You love Mick, don't you?"

Christa lowered her head. "Yes."

"Then remember the passage in First John. 'There is no fear in love.'" She knelt in front of Christa. "Don't let fear dictate your life, darlin', because you just might miss the greatest blessing ever."

There was a knock on her office door.

Christa looked up as Paisley stood. "Come on in, Patsy."

"This just came for you and I was instructed to give it to you right away." She placed square gift box on the desk.

Christa eyed her assistant manager. "Who's it from?"

Instead of responding, Patsy merely clamped her lips together and closed the door on her way out.

Christa looked from the silver-colored box to her friends.

"Well, open it already." Rae stood to join Laurel and Paisley around the desk.

Christa lifted the lid. Inside was a note card. When she lifted it out, there was a key on a heart-shaped chain beneath it with a tag that read The Gebhardt Building.

Her breath caught in her throat as she opened the card. "The key to your success. Check it out." She glanced at each of her friends, excitement welling inside her.

"Well, don't just sit there," said a grinning Rae. "Let's go."

They made their way out of the store and to the building next door like a bunch of giddy schoolgirls.

Christa paused to take in the narrow building with a blue door situated between two picture windows. A week ago, this was what she wanted. But now?

"Don't keep us waiting," Laurel said. "Unlock the door."

With trembling hands, Christa finally managed to do just that. Inside the building, century-old longleaf pine flooring stretched front to back while exposed brick walls climbed to meet the original tin ceiling. It was even better than she remembered.

Lowering her gaze, she nearly lost her footing when she spotted the path of red rose petals that wove through a series of floor easels that held large photos of her, Mick and Sadie.

After a moment, a gentle shove urged her forward. "Check it out, darlin'."

She glanced back at Paisley. "Did you know about this?"

"No, but I wish I had."

Christa moved past the images of the three of them in the ice storm, with the calf and around the campfire. The final picture sat atop a tall pedestal table and was of her and Mick beside the cow pond. Sadie had taken it on their last night together. A night that had held so much promise.

Her gaze fell to the bouquet of red roses, then continued to a velvet box beside a note that read, *I want to make all of your dreams come true.*

A sound had her looking up, and she drew in a sharp breath when she saw Mick moving toward her, looking finer than any man had a right to. His hair had been trimmed, he was clean shaven and he wore a pair of medium wash jeans and that black pearl-snap shirt she liked so much.

Could her heart beat any faster without exploding?

He stopped beside her, his smile tremulous as he took hold of her hands. "Christa, you brought color into my camo world and made it fuller, richer and more beautiful than I ever thought it could be." He looked away for a moment and swallowed before meeting her gaze. "I know I messed up. But if you could find it in your heart to forgive me, I'd like nothing more than to spend the rest of my life making you smile. I love you, Christa, with every fiber of my being." Letting go of her hands, he reached around her to retrieve the box. Then he opened the lid to reveal a glistening solitaire ring before dropping to one knee. "Will you marry me?"

If she thought she was giddy before… "Yes!"

Looking up at her, he appeared shocked. "Really?"

She set her hands on his cheeks. "Really."

Standing, he pulled her to him and kissed her with an intensity she'd never felt before. How could she have doubted this man? He was as honest as the day was long. Steady and unchanging. And he was hers.

But—she abruptly pulled away. "Where's Sadie?"

"Stand by." He pulled out his phone and sent off a text before looking at her. "I wanted to make sure you said yes first."

A second later, Bum's daughter Sandy approached the door with Sadie. The child that had stolen Christa's heart was wearing her prettiest dress and those pink cowboy boots.

She cautiously entered the space, scanning the faces until she found her uncle and Christa.

Mick practically beamed. "She said yes!"

Sadie's face lit up as she rushed into his waiting arms. "See, I tolded you."

"You sure did, princess." He slipped his other arm around Christa's waist, looking deep into her eyes as he tugged her close. "You sure did."

Across the room, Rae cleared her throat. "So, does this mean you're not leaving us?"

As Mick slid the ring on Christa's finger, she said, "Not on your life. Bliss is where I belong, and Bliss is where I'm staying."

The happiest day of Mick's life was about to collide with the scariest day of his life.

Deciding they had no reason to wait, he and Christa had acquired their marriage license first thing Monday morning and were married Thursday morning, only hours before he was due in court. The ceremony had taken place at Bliss Community Church, with only their closest friends and Sadie in attendance. He'd never been happier.

But now, as they posed for wedding photos among the magnolia and live oak trees on the courthouse square, the weight of this afternoon's hearing threatened to choke him. There was no telling how many lawyers the Sandersons would have with them. Probably a whole army.

"These are some great shots." Birds chirped overhead as the photographer looked up from her camera and smiled at Mick, Christa and Sadie. "The three of you are such an adorable family."

Her statement only intensified the knot in his stomach. Then he spotted the white Mercedes SUV pulling into a parking space along the square. Moments later, Chuck and Belita Sanderson emerged.

His hold on Christa's waist tightened.

"What is it?" She looked up at him, then followed his stare. Squeezing his arm, she whispered, "David took down Goliath with a slingshot and a stone. This is God's battle, Mick."

He peered down at her, fully aware of how blessed he was to have her at his side. She looked so beautiful in her wedding dress. Not the typical gown with a train and a veil, but the ivory knee-length dress with sheer sleeves and lace was no less stunning. "I'm so glad I married you."

"Me, too." She smiled.

"Sadie, sweetheart."

He turned to see Chuck and Belita coming toward them. Belita's arms were wide, her gaze fixed on her granddaughter.

Out of the corner of his eye, he saw Christa whisper something to Sadie before the child started toward her grandmother. Though Sadie appeared somewhat nervous, she earnestly hugged the woman.

Mick and Christa had talked with her several times over the past few days, carefully explaining that her grandparents wanted her to live with them. At first she'd stomped her foot, stating emphatically that she didn't want to live with them. Thankfully, she seemed to have calmed some since. Though there was no telling what things might look like if she was forced to leave with them today.

"Mick." Chuck continued toward them.

Mick took hold of Christa's hand as Belita drew nearer with Sadie in tow. "Chuck. Belita." He nodded. "This is my wife, Christa."

Their wary gazes narrowed.

"Wife?" Chuck winced.

Mick glanced at his watch. "As of about an hour-and-a-half ago."

Belita pressed a hand to her chest, her blue eyes raking over Christa. "My, isn't that convenient."

"Sadie's told me a lot about you." Christa smiled graciously at the couple.

"Yes, I'm sure she has." Releasing Sadie, Belita turned. "Come along, Chuck."

Christa's hazel eyes widened as she faced Mick. Placing her mouth beside his ear, she said, "That woman is scary."

He chuckled, then whispered back, "Not near as scary as you'd be if she did anything to hurt Sadie." Looking up, he saw Cole crossing the courthouse lawn.

"I hear congratulations are in order." The attorney eyed the two of them.

"Yes, sir," Mick said. "Let's just hope it continues."

They said goodbye to their friends then Mick knelt in front of Sadie. "You have fun with Miss Laurel and Sarah-Jane, and we'll see you in a bit."

She hugged his neck. "I love you, Uncle Mickey."

Uncertainty had him battling his emotions as he hugged her back. "I love you, too, princess."

Christa gave Sadie a squeeze, then they

watched until Laurel drove away before heading into the courthouse.

Inside the courtroom, Mick and Cole sat at a long wooden table to the front and right of the judge's bench while the Sandersons sat opposite with, to Mick's surprise, only one lawyer. Christa, Bum and Sadie's teacher, Tammy Shelton, were all slated to testify and sat in the gallery behind Mick.

He swiped his damp palms along his trousers. For the second time this week, he had a lot at stake. He could only pray that today's outcome would go as well as his proposal to Christa had.

"All rise."

The judge entered the courtroom and wasted no time getting down to business. The Sandersons' attorney laid out their case first, going on about how Sadie would want for nothing with her grandparents.

"She will have access to the best caretakers, schools and health care," the man said.

Mick shook his head in disbelief. The caretakers and schools were the main reasons Kyle *didn't* want Sadie with his parents.

Next, the man revealed that the Sandersons had, indeed, hired a private investigator. Though aside from Sadie's sprained arm and the fact that Christa had stayed with them, there wasn't much else.

"Your Honor," their lawyer said in closing, "my clients are still grieving the loss of their only child. Now they're in danger of losing their grandchild, too."

Mick straightened. Could that be what this was all about? They thought he'd keep Sadie from them. Had he done something to make them believe that?

Finally it was Cole's turn. He called Sadie's teacher first and the judge asked her some questions about Sadie, what her observations were of the child's relationship with Mick and if she'd ever seen the Sandersons before.

Bum was the next to take the stand, where he spoke about Mick's character, telling them he'd known Mick since he was born.

Finally Christa took the stand.

"How long have you known Mr. Ashford?" the judge asked.

"Approximately three years."

"What can you tell the court about his relationship with the child?"

"Mick has gone out of his way to help Sadie adjust." She looked at Mick. "I'll never forget the day he came into the hardware store, wanting this ugly pink paint for Sadie's bedroom so she would feel at home. I managed to talk him out of that particular color but have seen how willing he is to adapt to Sadie's needs. He's attentive and conscientious. Sure, he's struggled some, but he's learning."

"And how does Sadie respond to Mr. Ashford?"

"She adores him. I've seen them work together, celebrate together and grieve together. Just the way a family should." Again, her gaze turned to Mick. "And I'm so thankful they asked me to be a part of it."

The love Mick felt for this amazing woman swelled within him. Knowing how much she believed in him made him want to be a better man.

"The court will recess for ten minutes." The judge stood and left the room.

Mick briefly thanked Tammy and Bum for their input before pulling his wife aside. "I love you."

"I love you, too."

He glanced toward the Sandersons, noting that their attorney had left the room. "I'll be right back." He continued to the other table.

This time when they looked up at him, there was something different. Instead of two people ready to attack, he saw only fear. Fear of losing someone they loved.

He cleared his throat. "You know, nothing or no one can ever change the fact that you are Sadie's grandparents. And I want you to know that no matter what happens here today, I would never stand in the way of your relationship with her."

The older couple looked at each other. Belita sent her husband the slightest hint of a nod before Chuck turned to him.

"We appreciate that, Mick. Sadie is all we have left of Kyle."

"I'm aware of that. We've all suffered a great loss."

"Mick." Cole tugged at his elbow, noting that the judge was returning.

With a nod toward the Sandersons, Mick returned to his seat.

The judge sat behind the bench and stared out over the small group. "These types of cases are never easy. Decisions are made based on what's been presented here today."

Mick's breathing intensified. His heart felt as though it was in his throat.

"That said, after listening to both sides, the court finds it is in the best interest of Sadie Louise Sanderson to remain in the custody of Michael John Ashford. Court is adjourned."

As the gavel came down, Mick breathed a sigh of relief. *Thank You, God. You are, indeed, my defender.*

Mick again thanked Cole, Bum and Tammy for their help. "I hope y'all will join us across the street at Rae's, because you've certainly played a part in making this an extra special celebration."

After shaking their hands, he found his wife and hugged her like crazy. "You were amazing up there. I couldn't have done this without you."

Pulling back, she looked him in the eye. "Yes, you could. You love Sadie and you would do anything for her."

"I reckon you're right about that." He couldn't stop grinning at the beautiful woman before him. "She's ours." Resting his forehead against Christa's, he said, "I am so glad this is over."

"Me, too. Because we have a party to get to." She tilted her head to look at him. "I contacted Laurel and she said they're already over at Rae's."

"Good, then we can tell Sadie." He turned to look for the Sandersons, but they were already gone. And the disappointment Mick felt surprised him.

Taking Christa by the hand, they made their way downstairs and outside where Sadie waited with Laurel.

Mick scooped his precious niece into his arms. "Princess, I sure hope you like living at the ranch, 'cause that's where you're going to stay."

"Really?"

"Really."

She hugged his neck so hard he could barely breathe. "Now I can move into Miss Christa's house with you, and Dixie will be my dog, too."

He kissed her cheek. "She sure will." Wrapping his free arm around Christa, he kissed her, too. "Thank you. For everything."

"Hey, it's what we wives do." She winked.

Spotting the Sandersons midway across the square, he set Sadie on the ground. "Christa, watch Sadie for me." He caught up with the Sandersons a few seconds later. Stepping in front of them, he said, "Since you had to drive all the way to Bliss, you're welcome to stick around for a while." He motioned for Christa to join them. "We're about to head across the street for our wedding reception. Would you like to join us? You could spend some time with Sadie."

"We wouldn't want to impose," Chuck was quick to say.

"You're not imposing." He reached for Christa's hand as she approached. "You're invited."

They looked at each other and for the first time, Mick saw what looked like a genuine smile from Belita as she watched Sadie.

"What do say, Sadie? Would you like Grandpa and me to come to Mick and—" She glanced at Christa. "I'm sorry."

"Christa."

"That's right," Belita continued. "Would you like us to come to Mick and Christa's party?"

"Yes, please." In true Sadie fashion, she took hold of her grandmother's hand. "But we need to hurry before they eat all the cake."

"Oh, my." Belita laughed. "We can't let that happen."

While Chuck followed after them, Mick faced his wife. "I hope you don't mind?"

"Not at all. But we should go." She started to walk away, but he drew her back.

"Not so fast, Mrs. Ashford." Pulling her to him, he cupped her cheek. "You're the best thing that's ever happened to me. It may have taken us a long time to find each other, but there won't be a day that goes by that I won't thank God that we did."

She stared into his eyes, her fingers combing the hair at the back of his neck. "Thank you for not giving up on me. For giving me the courage to love again."

Mick kissed his wife, feeling more alive than he had in a long time. He had a family once again. One that had been born out of a terrible tragedy. But together they would press on, in love and by the grace of God.

* * * * *

Dear Reader,

Have you ever had a preconceived notion about someone, only to find out they're nothing like you expected once you had the opportunity to get to know them? Mick and Christa had been little more than acquaintances for three years until they were suddenly thrust together. And the common goal of helping a child brought out the best in both of them.

I hope you enjoyed this story as much as I did. Mick and Christa's tale was definitely one of my favorites. There's nothing more tender than a rough and tumble fellow falling prey to the whims of a little girl. So, naturally, Christa never stood a chance.

Yes, love does blossom between the most unexpected people sometimes. And those are often stories that are the most fun to write.

We're only halfway through my Bliss, Texas, series. Up next is Paisley's story, and I cannot wait to see what is in store for the beautiful redhead who's suffered such a great loss.

Until then, I would love to hear from you. You can contact me via my website, mindyobenhaus.com, or you can snail-mail me c/o Love Inspired Books, 195 Broadway, 24th Floor, New York, NY 10007.

Wishing you many blessings,
Mindy

Get 4 FREE REWARDS!

We'll send you 2 FREE Books plus 2 FREE Mystery Gifts.

Love Inspired Suspense books showcase how courage and optimism unite in stories of faith and love in the face of danger.

FREE
Value Over
$20

HARLEQUIN SELECTS COLLECTION

19 FREE BOOKS IN ALL!

From Robyn Carr to RaeAnne Thayne to Linda Lael Miller and Sherryl Woods we promise (actually, GUARANTEE!) each author in the Harlequin Selects collection has seen their name on the *New York Times* or *USA TODAY* bestseller lists!